The Adventures
of
Dagobert Trostler

Balduin Groller

Kazabo Publishing

Table of Contents

FOREWORD

Dagobert Trostler, the Austro-Hungarian Empire's answer to Sherlock Holmes, was the creation of Adalbert Goldscheider, better-known by his pen name, Balduin Groller. Groller, an interesting character in his own right, was a writer and journalist as well as the first President of the Austrian Olympic Committee.

Groller was very familiar with Viennese high society and it shows in his Dagobert Trostler stories. Turn-of-the-century Vienna was a very different place than turn-of-the-century London and, so, Dagobert Trostler is a very different sort of investigator than Sherlock Holmes.

Sherlock Holmes is a loner and a misanthrope with a nonetheless strong sense of duty and an even stronger sense of justice. Holmes lives by a clear and inflexible code. Criminals must be punished. Order must be preserved. In this, at least, Sherlock Holmes is a product of Victorian society.

Dagobert Trostler, by contrast, is an entirely social animal. Trostler, too, lives by a moral code, but a far more nuanced and flexible one. For Trostler, exacting justice often takes a back seat to preserving reputations. If the cost of avoiding a scandal is allowing the miscreant to escape, then, for Herr Dagobert, that's a small price to pay. Even minor social embarrassment must be avoided. In one of his adventures, Trostler employs his considerable skills to apprehend a wanted criminal but without causing an unpleasant scene at a party.

Perhaps even more interesting than his relationship with crime is his attitude regarding women. While Trostler always avoids scandal, what constituted a scandal in *fin de siècle* Vienna was very different than what constituted a scandal in *fin de siècle* London. There is nothing in these stories that the modern reader will find at all shocking but a great deal that a Victorian Londoner would. One wonders if this louche approach to "propriety" explains why these stories where not published in English shortly after they appeared.

Like Sherlock Holmes, Dagobert Trostler is a product of his society. But, unlike Victorian London, that society is largely unknown to us. Victorian London lives on in the popular imagination. But the Austro-Hungarian Empire and the social system it developed over six hundred years perished in the wreck of World War I and has largely vanished. For most of us, ancient Rome is more familiar. This is a shame because, in many ways, Vienna in 1900 was a far more exciting, congenial and intriguing place than was London. We hope you enjoy this glimpse of Viennese society in the last days of the Empire.

Chiara Giacobbe

The Fine Cigars

1.

After dinner, they went into the smoking room. This was an iron law, and could not be otherwise. The two gentlemen might have preferred to sit at the table to smoke their cigars in comfort, having enjoyed the culinary masterpieces, but that was not possible, absolutely not possible. They had known this for a long time, and now the departure and exodus seemed to them quite self-evident. The beautiful housewife had made it so. In her house, smoking was allowed only in the smoking room. There, she even took part occasionally and smoked a cigarette herself in company, but for all the other rooms—she imposed this—there was the strictest ban on smoking.

Mrs. Violet Grumbach, like any self-respecting person, took as much care over her character as her apartment. Just as her outward appearance was staged with every conceivable care, with taste and good calculation, so too was the apartment. The decor was modern and expensive, everything was spick-and-span and positively sparkled in cleanliness. Yet, it is sometimes still said that former artists generally don't make good housewives!

Frau Violet had been an actress. Not one of the very foremost, but certainly one of the prettiest. Even now, all that was true! She was an exceptionally attractive woman. A little under medium height, her figure pleasingly roundish and full, already considerably more developed than at the time of her active artistry. The pale blonde hair, always elaborately ordered, bright, sparkling gray eyes, delicately drawn, soft red lips, and a piquant, pert little snub nose which still gave the round little face a kind of childish expression. All in all, a very pleasant ensemble.

At meals, she loved always to appear in a specially chosen attire. There were no children in the house, so she had time to enhance life, and overall, she had a very good way of enhancing life. She adorned herself and her surroundings. It is thus understandable that she didn't want to expose her curtains, her lace and doilies, her ceilings, and her silk carpets to the evil effects of tobacco.

Today, only one guest was present, the old friend of the house, Dagobert Trostler, and he was so at home at the Grumbach's that absolutely no bother was made on his account. If Frau Violet had once again attended elaborately to her attire, it was not actually meant for him. Once upon a time, it was customary even when she dined alone with her husband. Now, at the very most, some nuances were added on account of the guest. Thus, the heart-shaped cutout of her white lace blouse, which gave the observer some views and insights, and the half-length lace sleeves, which gave the plumpish forearms that delicately tapered to fine wrists and pretty little hands the desired scope.

Mr. Andreas Grumbach, owner of a large and very lucrative jute weaving mill, president of the General Construction Company Bank, and also bearer of numerous titles and honors, was considerably older than his wife—around twenty years or so— and if one were denied calculating the age of the ladies with too much brutal accuracy, it may be revealed with him. He might have seen fifty-three or fifty-four springs, but he looked even older than he was. His beautiful dark-brown, smooth-brushed hair proved nothing. He could have had his hair dressed professionally. His sideburns already shimmered strongly silver, and yet his chin had been shaved in the attempt to look a little younger and not to let the silvery blessing grow excessively.

Dagobert Trostler, his old friend, had by no means been sanguine when Grumbach, pursuing the late stirrings of love, had brought home the actress Violet Moorlank as his wedded spouse about six years ago. But nothing could be done about it, and finally Dagobert was proven wrong all along. A quite acceptable and respectable household developed of it. The marriage turned into a very happy one.

Dagobert himself had remained a bachelor. He was a fully-fledged man-about-town with a noticeably thinning crown and a St Peter's style tuft of hair. His Socratic face was enlivened by two dark, expressive eyes. Now he had only two great passions, music and criminology. His great fortune allowed him to devote himself to these two very divergent hobbies without any other anxiety. He had an enjoyable and creative relationship with music. His friends claimed that it was the stronger of his two talents. He, too, had known Violet when she was still a member of the theater, and when one or another of her roles required that she sing some songs, he was the one who had rehearsed her. As an amateur, of course. He remained an amateur, passionate dilettante, gentleman-rider in all the fields of activity in which he was engaged. He had, however, had some musical success with that arrangement. Indeed, in this way, he sometimes succeeded in smuggling one or another of his own compositions into the public as contributions.

As far as his criminological inclinations were concerned, they first expressed themselves in the fact that he leaned toward talking about murder-robberies and halfway respectable embezzlements. He was convinced he could have been a first-rate detective inspector, and stiffly asserted that if worst came to the worst, he would be well able to earn his bread as a detective. His friends made fun of him for it. Not that they would have doubted his talent. He had often enough provided convincing proof of that. They found only his passion for making unnecessary trouble for himself peculiar. For his hobby brought him not only numerous inconveniences, but also occasionally entangled him in really quite dangerous situations. If there was a crowd of people somewhere, he was certainly there, too, but not with an interest in the current proceedings, whatever they might be. He would watch out for pickpockets and endeavored to observe them at work and catch them in the act. For this reason, he was not infrequently involved in risky complications, but he still succeeded in delivering many a pilferer into police hands. Thus, he also loved to do research into dark crimes on his own initiative, and so it was that he brought all sorts of trouble down on his own head, had dealings in court at every moment, or was summoned to the police, to whom his private efforts had sometimes become uncomfortable. But all this gave him pleasure. He was an amateur after all.

So, one went to the smoking room.

The two gentlemen sat down at the little smoker's table near the window. Frau Violet took a seat on a small, padded bench—a very charming piece of furniture—which stretched from the high and finely structured chimney to the door, and there filled the space very becomingly. The fireplace stood in a corner, creating a very cozy little spot.

Grumbach took a cigar box from the smoking table, not at random. There were several of them there, and he had chosen carefully. He opened it and was about to pass the cigars to Dagobert as he trimmed.

"I don't know," he said thoughtfully, "there must still be a connoisseur in my house for precisely this sort of cigar. It would not be bad taste: they cost a florin apiece!"

"Do you notice disappearances?" asked Dagobert.

"I think I notice them," replied Grumbach.

"Nothing is stolen in our house," said Frau Violet, defending her honor as housewife.

"Thank God, no!" Grumbach replied. "And yet—certainly, I can't state it for a fact—but it seems to me as if only two cigars were missing from the top yesterday, and today there are eight or nine missing."

"Your own fault," remarked Dagobert. "You must simply keep them under lock and key!"

"One should be able to leave a thing lying around free in one's own home!"

"Perhaps you are mistaken?" suggested Frau Violet.

"It would not be impossible, but I don't believe it. Well, it isn't a misfortune precisely, but it is disturbing."

"It should not be difficult to get to the bottom of the matter, however," remarked Dagobert, in whom the detective passion began to stir.

"The simplest thing will be to follow your advice, Dagobert. Lock it. That's the best protection."

"That would not be interesting enough for me," was the reply. "You must catch the marten!"

"Am I supposed to be on the lookout for days on end? It'll cost me a lot less if I buy a few more cigars."

"But you must know who has access to the room."

"I stand for my servant. He takes nothing!"

"And I for my maid," Frau Violet added hurriedly. "She's been with me since I was a child, and not a pin has ever gone missing!"

"Even better," continued Dagobert. "Do you think there are daily disappearances?"

"God forbid! That's all I need! Last week I thought I had noticed it, and then perhaps in the previous week too."

The subject dropped. They spoke a little while more about the events of the day that occupied public opinion. Then the host and hostess rose to make their final preparations to attend the opera. It was their day for the box, Wednesday, and Dagobert was supposed to make one of the party, as usual. Such an old acquaintance and familiar friend of the house could be left alone for a little quarter of an hour, without awkwardness.

Frau Violet, joking, said that it must even be welcome to remain alone for a while, since he could now cogitate undisturbed on the gloomy problem of where the disappearing cigars had got to. He would surely work it out, as a master detective!

It would not have taken this mocking appeal to remind him of his hobby. He had already quietly decided to discover the perpetrator, and now he welcomed the chance to look around the scene of the crime undisturbed. The case was in fact quite insignificant, but what does an amateur not do to stay in training? He takes an opportunity like this.

When he was alone, he sat down in his armchair and began to think, for the story was not quite so simple. The last offense had been committed the day before. He assessed the cigar box and the smoking table. There was nothing to discover. It was simply disgusting what kind of cleanliness prevailed in the house, how things were tidied up and wiped down daily! How was a person expected to discover a fingerprint on the wood frame of the smoking table, which the red fabric of the ledge bordered? The frame probably was not dusty yesterday either, and since then it had been ridiculously wiped and polished again. How was a man supposed to make fingerprint studies?

Okay. Forget that.

Four electric lamps now lit the room. He turned the other eight on with a knob. Radiant light filled the room, and now he examined further. He paced the room in all directions, and sent a searching glance everywhere, unable to find any clue.

Then he sat again at the smoking table. It was clear that this had to form the center of the inquiries. However much he peered, no trace and no *corpus delicti* was discovered, But, just as he was about to resume his pacing, he noticed something. Nestled in the narrow gap between the cloth and wood frame of the smoking table, and projecting over it, was a hair, dark and shiny, not long—perhaps five centimeters, straightened—but it had the tendency to form a circle.

Dagobert ran his hand over the cloth, the frame, and the gap where the hair was. The hair bent and remained stuck. So, it had also been able to withstand polishing and dusting. On the other hand, the way things were cleaned here—absolutely disgusting—it was probably safe to assume that this resistance would hardly be permanent. Multiple attacks would probably sweep the hair away. It was quite possible, indeed probable, that it only got stuck yesterday.

He thought for a moment about calling in the servant to ascertain whether someone who was not part of the household had entered the room today, perhaps to get out of him who had been there yesterday, but he pushed the thought away immediately. Of course he wanted to, had to spy, but not with the servants! That could lead to foolish talk, and he was guilty of a certain regard for the house of his best friend.

So, he lifted the hair with his fingertips and put it with extreme care in his billfold. Then he continued his research. He had a good look around the entire room again. There was hardly anything more to be learned. The lighting was so bright that he was unlikely to miss anything. Up on the smooth, polished surface of the black-marble fireplace mantle, he noticed a small, dark lump interrupting the sharp straight line. Was it worth examining? For a detective, everything is worth it, anything can be worthwhile.

He pulled up a leather chair and climbed on it. A cigar butt, about four centimeters long. A very light layer of dust on the polished ledge. If only the housewife knew! It had not been wiped today. The servant had made himself comfortable. Probably he only wiped every second or third day. The thin layer of dust was not older than that. Neither was the stub. A smoker could judge that. And another thing: there was no trace of a hand or finger on the dust surface. The ledge, therefore, had not been dusty when the ash tray was put there. It should therefore—therefore, it was put down yesterday.

Dagobert examined the stub. It came from the type of cigar in question.

Now Dagobert got off the chair, put the carefully wrapped stub in his pocket, extinguished the surplus lamps, and then, when the time came, went to the opera.

2.

Grumbach had already forgotten the whole cigar matter the next day. The busy factory owner and merchant had other things to think about. He didn't come back to it later, because there was no reason to do so. The matter was still not done with, however.

Dagobert let almost a whole week pass before he returned to Grumbach's home. The last time he had been there on a Wednesday, and he didn't show up again until the following Tuesday evening. Frau Violet received him in the smoking room. Dinner was over, and with the coffee he was supposed to have with her, she liked to smoke a cigarette.

"Have I arrived inopportunely, ma'am?" he began the conversation.

"You are always welcome, Herr Dagobert," she replied amiably, but she seemed to be a little bit sheepish as she sat down on the fireplace bench.

"I only meant," he went on innocently, "because I had anticipated that I would not meet your husband at home."

"Certainly, Tuesday is his club day. He is never at home then. All the more pleasant for me to have company."

"It would have been possible, however, that madame had already provided herself with different society, and that I might only have been an inconvenience."

"You are never an inconvenience, Herr Dagobert," she assured him eagerly, then steered the conversation a different direction, by attacking his weak side and beginning to tease him with his detective passion.

"Now, have you not discovered the nefarious cigar marten yet?" she asked with cheerful mockery.

"Do not mock too early, madame."

"My God, a few cigars can easily go missing without one knowing where they've gone. You should simply not investigate. The next thing will be to suspect the servant. He is certainly innocent, but once suspicion is aroused—my husband is very strict—the poor devil could easily lose his livelihood."

"We shall soon see for ourselves," replied Dagobert, pressing the electric switch.

Frau Violet was frightened by his forwardness and made a movement to hold him back, but it was already too late. In the next moment, the servant was in the room awaiting orders.

"You, my dear Franz," began Dagobert, "Will you be

so good as to get me a cab, in about an hour."

"Very well, sir!"

"Here, dear friend, for your effort a fine cigar!" Dagobert reached for the little box.

"I beg your pardon, sir, I don't smoke."

"Oh, nonsense, Franz," said Dagobert. "Now get out your cigar box. We want to fill it properly." And he now reached into the little box with his whole hand.

Franz laughed broadly at the joke, and assured him that he was not a smoker.

"Well, that's all right," remarked Dagobert affably, "then we will still settle things between ourselves. You should not miss out."

The servant bowed and left the room noiselessly.

"You see, madame," resumed Dagobert. "It was not him."

Now it was up to Frau Violet to laugh brightly.

"If that's your entire trick, Dagobert, then you had better go to the bottom of the class! Indeed, I don't say that it was him—it certainly was not. But even if he had been guilty, do you really believe he would fallen into this clumsy trap?"

"Who says, Frau Violet, that this is all I have up my sleeve? I only wanted to demonstrate to you that he could not be the culprit."

"Because you believe everything he says at once. You are naïve, Dagobert."

"It was pointless for me to summon him. I only wanted to accomplish his salvation before you. Actually, in quite a superfluous way, for you, too, are convinced of his innocence, and thus we could regard the matter as closed."

"Dagobert, you know more than you say."

"I will tell you everything, if it interests you, my dear."

"I am very interested."

"Would it be better not to talk about it at all any longer?"

"Indeed, why should it be better, Dagobert?"

"I just thought—because I know everything."

"All the better. Let me hear what you have found out."

"It is, of course, possible that I am mistaken in the details, then you will be able to correct me."

"I?" She looked at him magnificently.

"You, madame. It is also possible that I will make a fool of myself—I don't believe it, but it's possible. You must take into account that I have been solely dependent on my reasoning, and I have, quite naturally, scorned to pump your servants for information."

"Not such a long introduction, Dagobert. Get to the point, please."

"Fine, I'll show my cards. You remember, my dearest, that last Wednesday I heard about the disappearances for the first time. Five minutes later I had the exact description of the person."

"How did you get that, then?"

"The exact description of the person, the smoker. I think we will stay with this designation and avoid the odious expression thief or even cigar thief. The cigars, indeed, were not stolen, but merely smoked without the master knowing it. The smoker is, therefore, a tall young man, a head taller than I am, with a well-groomed black beard and splendid teeth."

"How do you know?"

"I'll tell you everything, madame. By the way, I hope to see the correctness of the personal description I've supplied strikingly confirmed today. Namely, I reckon on the fact that the excellent young man will soon grant us the honor of his company. I have already filled the box with his favorite cigars."

Then the door opened, and the servant entered with the message that the carriage had been ordered for the gracious lord, and that it would drive up punctually at the appointed time. Then he addressed to the housewife the question of whether he was now "allowed to go." Permission was granted, and he withdrew with a submissive bow of thanks.

"Franz is actually a theater fiend," explained Frau

Violet. "Once a week he must go to the theater, and I prefer to give him Tuesday evenings off, when my husband isn't at home, and he can be most easily dispensed with."

"Oh, I see," replied Dagobert thoughtfully. "Well, that is indeed fair enough."

"Do not let that distract you, dear Dagobert," continued Frau Violet. "You owe me the explanation of how you got to that description of the person."

"I had a few minutes to investigate on Wednesday, when you and your husband retired to prepare for the theater. The matter might perhaps have become difficult if I had not found any clues on the scene."

"And you found some?"

"Yes. A hair in the gap of the smoking table, and an ash tray at the fireplace."

"But they could have been lying here and there for a long time!"

"I had my reasons to believe that they were actually *corpora delicti* and had only arrived there the day before. I then examined the two objects at home, the hair microscopically."

"And the result?"

"A perfectly satisfying one. The hair pointed to a perpetrator with a beautiful black beard. Natural black, no trace of artificial dye. So, an old man isn't our smoker. I can even say that it is a young man. For the hair was soft, pliant and supple. Not exactly the first fluff, but still delicate. It would have been coarser and more bristly, if a razor had prevailed there for many years past. The young man also puts something on his beard, for under the microscope the hair showed a trace of Brilliantine. This is a quite harmless, cosmetic remedy, but one must be a little vain to apply it. As you know the perpetrator, my dear, you will indeed be able to judge whether my assumption is correct or erroneous."

"I think you've gotten carried away by an obsession."

"Possibly. But that isn't important. Let's move on. Up here, on the fireplace ledge, lay the ash tray."

"To what conclusions did it lead you?"

"First of all, I was pleased to see that the cigar type was the right one. Further conclusions were self-evident. Now allow me to return to your servant. I mention here something virtually in conclusion, which I thought and which I actually started with. Not for no reason did I call him in. You should take another look at him. So, the man is blond, and his face, as befitting a proper servant, also serving at the table, is shaved smooth. In addition, not befitting a proper servant, and as you could see for yourself when he grinned so kindly at us, he has very bad teeth. Finally, you could see that his stature is a rather small one. He's a little smaller than I am, and we have established that the unknown perpetrator has a black beard, has very good teeth, and is a head taller than I am."

"We have not yet established this at all!"

"Then we'll do so immediately. The tip of the cigar had not been cut off with a knife, but had been bitten off cleanly and smoothly. This means good teeth. Now we've got that straight. Now his unusual height must be proven. Nothing easier than that. Let us reproduce the situation, my gracious one—actually not necessary at all. Because it is already established. You at your preferred spot, I leaning against the fireplace opposite you, at a respectful distance, but still close enough for our conversation. The prospect, which I enjoy almost from a bird's eye view, is an enchanting one—you don't need to threaten, Frau Violet—an adorable one. I would not leave my happy observer post on a mere whim. But if I had to put away a cigar, I would have to go to the smoker's table, where the ashtrays stand, because I could not reach the ledge. It would be too high for me! There, now I have justified the person's description. Is it correct, my dear?"

"It is true," admitted Frau Violet, laughing. "I compliment you, Herr Dagobert. You are a terrible man, and I can see that it will be for the best if I make a comprehensive confession, or else God knows what you will believe in the end!"

"No confessions! I reject them. Confessions—of course I speak quite academically—can also be wrong. There have been legal executions on the basis of false confessions, and nothing gets my blood up more than the thought of a judicial murder. Besides, I don't need the confession. It cannot help me anymore. I am only an examining magistrate here, and I make no rulings. My task was to clarify the facts and prove the perpetrators. Whether this is confessed or denied in the final negotiation, I am not concerned."

"Good, so let us hear more!"

"So, I had to deduce further. The tall young man with the beautiful beard and the good teeth smoked his cigar here in your presence and provided you company. He chatted with you as I am now speaking with you. There could be no special secret behind it."

"Thank God that you don't think me capable of that at least, Dagobert!"

"That could not be behind it. We have known each other long enough—you are a clever woman. You know what's at stake, and you don't do stupid things."

"I thank you for your trust in my honor!"

"My trust is rock-solid, no less so my respect. But it isn't just that. I have open eyes and good ears. I myself would have noticed something, or some kind of talk would have come to me. None of any of this. You received a visit, which could not attract attention, otherwise it would have already been noticed. Why did it not attract attention? Because you often receive him. It had to have been a quite harmless visit. A circumstance, however, could make us wonder. From the explanations given by your husband, I was able to deduce that the cigars usually disappeared on Tuesday evening, at the time when he was at the club. What I didn't know, but what you indicated, is that on Tuesday your servant likes to attend the theater."

"I hope you will not draw your conclusions from this circumstance!"

"I don't think so. In fact, it seems to me that the young man appears quite frequently on the premises, but that on Tuesday he lingered a little longer and entertained the housewife."

"That is true, but I can assure that the conversations are quite harmless."

"I never doubted this, especially since the young man—how can I say? —is a little below your level."

"How did you sift that out, Dagobert?"

"It is self-explanatory, madame. Our friend Grumbach has not missed one or two cigars, but six or seven. You remember, according to him, two cigars had been missing from the top layer the day before. In any case, Grumbach took them out himself and thus half involuntarily got the impression presented by the inside of the box. One day later, it seemed to him as if eight or nine pieces were missing. Thus, the disappearance of six or seven pieces. However, one does not smoke six or seven heavy cigars during an hour's chat with the lady of the house, one smokes one. Two at most. Now it looks as if the mistress had encouraged the young man to take a few more cigars when he left."

"That's right, too. But it still does not follow that I, as you prefer to express it, should have entertained myself with someone at a level below my own."

"I beg your pardon, my dearest. For a proper social visit, the housewife might suggest one take along a cigar—one! Of course, without emphasis. To give a handful—or to take them—well, that indicates a certain social distance."

"You are really a pure detective superintendent, Dagobert!"

"At a distance, and yet with a certain sympathy."

"He is a very nice, amiable young man. Did you uncover anything else?"

"Oh, a whole bundle! I asked myself the question: What kind of young man can come into the house so often, perhaps daily, without any sort of notice? The answer was not difficult. It could only be an official from your husband's office, probably one who has the task of bringing the cashier's key or the daily report to the boss every day."

"Certainly, after business is closed, he brings home the daily report. My husband arranged it this way."

"Which he did very correctly. I know that, too, now, by the way. Because I was recently with your director."

"The things you get up to when you follow a clue!"

"Either one doesn't begin, my dearest, or one begins, but then one must go all the way to the end. Otherwise, it's pointless."

"And what did you accomplish with the director?"

"All I could wish for."

"Let me hear about it, Dagobert!"

"I told him that I had come to patronize a young man—only he was not to betray me to the chief. The director smiled. He knew quite well that if I wanted something from the boss, it would be approved from the outset. Possibly, I admitted, but I would rather not take advantage of our friendship by asking the chief directly. The director understood, or acted as if he understood, and offered himself at my disposal.

"'What's this about?' he asked.

"'You have a young man in the office,' I replied, 'Now, what's his name? I have such a hideous memory for names! Doesn't matter; it will come. I mean a remarkably tall young man with agreeable manners'— otherwise you wouldn't have liked him, my dearest— 'with a beautiful black beard and good teeth. In the evening, he usually delivers to the boss.'

"'Oh, that's our secretary, Sommer!' the director interrupted me.

"'Sommer, of course Sommer! How could the name slip my mind! You see, my dear Director, Sommer is indeed a very gifted person, but he's not at the right place in the office doing correspondence. He lacks the final precision and accuracy at work. On the other hand, he would be admirable for dealing with groups. I know that you have been looking for a suitable person for quite some time to head the sales branch in Graz. Wouldn't that be a good spot for Sommer?'

"The director slapped his forehead with his hand.

"'By goodness, that is an idea! There we are, searching until our eyes pop out of our heads and we have the man under our noses! Of course, Sommer is made for it! You haven't exercised patronage on him, rather, your suggestion does us a service. He'll go to

Graz. The matter is settled.'

"You see, my dearest, I was lucky enough to be able to play God a little."

"But Dagobert, how could you risk the assertion that the young man is not good for the office?"

"There was no risk in it. I relied on my little bit of psychology. The right office person is always more or less—to a certain extent—a pedant. His job requires him to exercise constant minute precision. Our friend is not a pedant. The right office person doesn't bite the tips of the cigars with his teeth, but cuts them neatly with a penknife or special tool that he carries securely with him if he is a cigar smoker. And there's something else the right office person doesn't do. He doesn't put cigar butts on marble fireplaces. Instead he strives to get to the ashtray and deposits the remains there, always striving to make sure that no trace of ash is left beside it. Our careless young friend, who is imprecise with a cigar stub, probably won't be very precise with office work. He doesn't have it in him!"

"And from this, you immediately concluded that he was the right man for sales?"

"Not only from that, but from the preference you have given him, my dearest. He must be very well-spoken, and he will probably also be a bit of a ladies' man. All this is very admirable when one has to make personal contact with customers."

"One thing you must tell me, Dagobert. You have tried to get rid of the young man because you were worried about my virtue?"

"But, Frau Violet! You know what trust I place in you! But as I knew that the disappearing cigars had passed through your hands, and that you were therefore keeping a secret from your husband, the smoker really had to disappear. It had to be so!"

"A secret, yes. That was the awkwardness for me. I didn't tell my husband immediately. I didn't think of it. And if he had made an issue of it, it would have raised doubts. It would have been embarrassing to me."

"That's just as I understood it, Madame. For me, by the way, my carriage must have arrived. If the young man should come to say goodbye, offer him a different variety of cigar for a change, and then this most important matter will be settled."

The Great Embezzlement

The most beautiful room in the Palace of the ABB—
it was always called the ABB everywhere, and everyone
knew at once that this meant the General Bank of
Construction—was the Bureau of the Director General.
He, a relatively young man of winning appearance, sat
before his impressive desk, and, with his well-groomed
and ring-clad hands, organized the letters and other
documents that had accumulated before him.

Then the door leading to the antechamber opened,
without having been knocked upon. He raised his head.
A pretty head. The eyes, looking startled by this rare but
improper interruption, were blue, and despite the
momentary resentment just expressed in them, an
observer and connoisseur of human nature and would
have recognized a ray of goodness and a certain almost
artistic enthusiasm. The shining brown head of hair was
parted, and a much lighter, indeed, decidedly blond
beard formed a quite remarkable contrast to it.

The head that was now poked around the door was
also very suitable for attracting attention. It was a
striking head that straddled faunal and biblical
appearance. The full face, framed by a black beard,
fairly sparkled with delight in the enjoyment of life,

while the little tuft of hair on the parting that evoked St. Peter, almost demanded a closer look to determine whether there was perhaps a corresponding halo to be discovered.

"Have you a quick half-hour for me, Mr. Ringhoff?" asked the man with the missing halo.

"Ah, Mr. Dagobert Trostler!" cried the Director General. Every trace of resentment had disappeared from his open face. "Do I have time? For you, always, even if you were not on my board of directors. What a pleasure! You were travelling, Mr. Trostler?"

"Yes indeed, several weeks, far away. In America, in fact."

"You don't say? A pleasure trip, Mr. Trostler?"

"Yes, it was extremely pleasurable, Herr Director General. I saw a lot."

"Did you see Yellowstone Park? It is supposed to be very interesting."

"Of course I visited Yellowstone."

"You must tell me all about it, Mr. Trostler."

"That's why I have come to you, Herr Director General."

They sat. Dagobert took a seat at the side of the desk with his back to the window. The Director General proffered him a cigar box, but Dagobert declined. As a smoker, he had his peculiarities. He had zeroed in on a particular variety, and from this he didn't deviate. He therefore only smoked his own cigars. In fact, he had not yet encountered a better Havana brand. Might the Director General just try and see for himself? Ringhoff helped himself, and once again encouraged his visitor to talk.

"I have a whole novel to tell you, and I must elaborate a little, but the story will interest you."

"I am interested in everything that concerns you, Mr. Trostler."

"Thank you very much. Tell me, dear Herr Director General, have you never wondered how I actually came to the ABB?"

"Why should I have wondered about it, Mr. Trostler?"

"Well, I don't understand anything about banking. That is, I didn't understand it, didn't have the slightest idea. Now, of course, after more than a year, I have properly familiarized myself."

"You came to us like the rest of the board of directors. You are a very wealthy man, Mr. Trostler, and as far as expertise is concerned, you very soon surpassed all the other gentlemen. There was absolutely no reason for me to wonder. But you wanted to tell me about your trip to America."

"I'm just getting to it. They are connected. First, you should know how and why I came to the ABB. I have always thought that everyone should have some kind of avocation, even a man like me, who is completely free and independent, and has neither bag nor baggage. So, I have two great passions. One is music. I don't know whether you have heard of my achievements in this field."

"Certainly, I've heard of them," lied the Director General firmly. "And—the other?"

"Yes, the other one—This is a very unusual thing. I am an amateur detective. You look surprised? I assure you, if one has a passion for the thing, and some talent, there is nothing more interesting."

"There is not much you can do with the first hobby here."

"But there is with the second! You remember the story. Indeed, how should you not? The ABB was founded, and my friend Grumbach, who was also the president of the Industrialists Club, was appointed president. This went quite well for a year, and then, you know, the cashier disappeared and with him three million crowns."

"It was a terrible blow!"

"My friend Grumbach, he's my most intimate friend, has bad luck in certain things. Hardly had he gotten used to being club president, he had another such unpleasant experience. The first time, he came to me, and I helped him out. Actually, I could tell you about that, too. It was a very fine racket, but that would lead us too far off point. So, this time he came to me again. If anyone could help, it was I. I had the case explained to me precisely, but there was not much to tell. The books were apparently in the greatest order, but the cashier and the money disappeared. Moreover, the cashier already had a head start of a substantial two weeks."

"Unfortunately, I remember all too clearly."

"He had gone on his vacation unchallenged, and when the great embezzlement emerged, every trace of his earthly pilgrimage had been wiped clean. Now I was to look for him."

"That was admittedly a lot to ask."

"Grumbach has a hard head in such matters. He wouldn't hear of reporting it to the authorities, and in this case, I could not disagree at all. Three million—that is, of course, a colossal amount, but the theft didn't have to ruin a bank with sixty million in paid-up capital. But dwindling public confidence would probably have destroyed it, if it had become known that, after a short period of existence, such a thing were possible."

"That was my opinion too, Mr. Trostler."

"I know. At the request of the president, therefore, the governing board decided to keep the fatal story completely secret, to repay the deficit for the administrative boards, and to replace it through their own means."

"After all, it was the best way out."

"Yes indeed. So now I was to help. I considered. First, I had to gain a completely clear insight into the ABB's workings. I thought of letting myself be employed as a clerk for this purpose, but soon rejected the idea. I didn't know enough about it, and that would have made me very conspicuous or suspicious. So, I had myself established as a board member. A board member does not make himself conspicuous when he knows nothing and cannot do anything."

The Director General smirked discreetly at this satirical remark and said airily, "Then you were not acting as a board member among us, but rather as a detective?"

"Naturally!"

"You will find it understandable, Mr. Trostler, that it must rankle me a little that I was told not a peep!"

"My dear Herr Director General, if the cat is going to catch mice, she will not tie a bell around her neck first. No one but the president knew about it, and you are now the first to whom I give this open-hearted information—if you are at all interested, which I cannot know."

"I am very interested!"

"Then I will continue to tell you about my—trip to America. First, I had to familiarize myself properly with the work. I did so, not too badly, as you will have the goodness to testify, Herr Director General."

"I can only say that you have become the soul of our administration, Mr. Trostler."

"Thank you, Herr Director General. Such a judgment from such a competent side must make me proud. My first concern was, therefore, aimed at making the repetition of such events impossible. You understand that such repetitions would inevitably have become a little tiring in the long run."

"I understand perfectly."

"This has been successful. I may say that the ABB's control systems have now become positively exemplary and instructive."

"They are and are recognized and imitated everywhere."

"My further concern was then the search for the missing cashier, and what was even more important, the vanished money. No easy thing. All effort had seemed hopeless from the outset. The man had disappeared without a trace and then—the lead!"

"And did you really succeed?"

"By God, I'm satisfied. At my request, I was supplied with a photograph of the vanished man and several samples of his handwriting. That was not much, was it? But what can one do if one does not have more? Then—but you must not laugh at me, Herr Director General! —I turned to a detective agency for information about the retired Mr. Josef Benk."

"There was, however, presumably little to be gained there for the present case."

"I admit it, and I knew it in advance, but I nonetheless learned a few details, which I otherwise I would have had to uncover myself, and which were necessary for my further investigations. The information was startling: Josef Benk Ritter von

Brenneberg—he had not made use of his noble title, and nothing was known about it at the bank. A former military officer, highly honorable character, absolutely trustworthy."

"That was always true of him among us until—"

"I know. So there was not much to begin with there. Even so, there were still some details that I could follow up on with further research. Now I thought of Isouard's criminological principle: *cherchez la femme.* You must not laugh at me again, Herr Director General. This is really a commonplace, and every layman would be expected to remember it, but that does not speak against its validity. In fact, criminal investigations are very often concerned with researching relationships with the eternal feminine. Believe me, Herr Director General. I am only an amateur detective, but I do claim the experiences of a professional. I am not of the opinion that the woman is always the instigator of the crime, or that most crimes are committed precisely for a woman's sake. I am only of the opinion that the female element signifies Siegfried's linden leaf for many criminals. You do understand me, Herr Director General? So, something like the Achilles' heel, or a gap in the armor, points to the place where they are mortal. Is this clear to you?"

"Absolutely."

"I think I'm decidedly in the right there. Samson would never have been restrained if he had not laid his head in Delilah's lap."

"And have you, Mr. Trostler, ferreted out such

important female relationships in this case too?"

"But of course! The fugitive had left behind a bride, a fine woman. A public school teacher—the most charming person you can imagine. She embodied grace, intelligence, and honor. No one in the world could have chosen better."

"And he left her disdainfully in the lurch?"

"Oh no! It was agreed that she should follow, once he had established a regular existence abroad."

"And has he been heard of since?"

"He has built up a fully ordered existence. This matter is completed perfectly smoothly. It was my pleasure to bring him the lovely bride—it was not acceptable to let her go alone across the sea—and I had the honor of being a witness at her marriage."

The Director General rose.

"Excuse me, Mr. Trostler," he said with a smile, "if I interrupt your story for a moment. I want merely to give a quick assignment in accounts, and then I will be able to follow your interesting report without disruption."

"You make the effort in vain, Herr Director General," replied Dagobert quietly, remaining seated. "You cannot get there. There are two detectives in the next room. That is, real police detectives, and not paltry amateurs like me. Needless to say, there are also two on the other side, in the antechamber. They are already making sure that we remain completely undisturbed.

They have strict orders not to let anyone in. Besides me, no one can leave this room without being immediately arrested. Do you wish to take the chance, Herr Director General?"

"No. What do you want from me?"

"Above all, I want to exercise full sincerity with you, not to trick you into sincerity. My position would be a very weak one if I had to rely on that. I don't need it. What I want to do is merely to convince you that I am holding you with iron clamps, as if you were clutched in a vice. Only when you are fully convinced of that can I reckon on that resolution from you, which, in my opinion, is still the only possible and reasonable one, and which I still need."

"What resolution?"

"We'll soon get to that. First, I have to convince you even more completely. You will allow me to be brief. I stayed with Mrs. von Benk as a lodger. She is the mother of our former treasurer, the widow of a lieutenant colonel. She lives in straightened circumstances, but it is a thoroughly honorable, morally clean milieu. So, as no master falls from heaven, no criminal falls from heaven, either. I was fairly out of composure, and my hope of finding the key to a criminal act was severely depressed. I had passed myself off as a piano teacher, and led a very solid and domestic life to acquire the confidence of the ladies. The ladies, for Benk's bride, Miss Ehlbeck, came to visit every day, and was, so to speak, part of the household. I managed to do this without any particular difficulty. I had taken care, as soon as I moved in, to drop the remark that I intended to stay only a few months until I had saved enough to be able to carry out my plan of resettlement in America. This harmless hint met its goal. Both Miss Ehlbeck, with whom I played duets very often, and the mother always came back to the subject of America. I proceeded systematically. From time to time, I sent various modest amounts to my address through postal money order, allegedly fees for my lessons, and asked Mrs. von Benk to set them aside for me. The money was better off with her than with me, and I wanted to keep it together for the journey. There was never any mention of the fugitive son, but neither was there ever a hint of anxiety or secrecy to be seen. Any uneasy consciences were decidedly absent, and it was clear that there could be no question of cognizance or complicity. But it seems, Herr Director General, that my talk affects you. Shall I perhaps pour you a glass of water?"

"Thank you, Mr. Trostler, please finish your story and make it short."

"I will. Finally, something arrived that I had awaited for a long time, a letter from America. You can imagine that I had kept a keen eye out for the postman. I saw the envelope and recognized the writing. I could easily have stolen the letter or read it secretly. I don't do such things. One has one's principles. Foreign letters were always sacred to me. I only requested the stamp for my collection. I already knew what I'd find. Of course, I was only interested in the postmark, and there I found confirmed what I had long already known. I had indeed long known the address, which you, too, know very well, Herr Director General: 'Mr. Brenneberg, 1400 Second Avenue South, Minneapolis, Minnesota, USA.'"

The Director General became even paler at these words. With a sudden desperate impulse, he put the key in his desk to pull it open.

"Do not be rash, Herr Director General," Dagobert commanded. "Leave the drawer quietly closed. It cannot help you. You have a revolver there, and I have a hand in my pocket, and in my hand a revolver, as well. I would be decidedly swifter, and besides, your revolver *was* loaded, mine *is*. I allowed myself, in my inspection, to empty all the cylinders and take the rounds with me."

"You worked with duplicate keys!"

"Naturally! I even got duplicates of the key to your main cash box."

"You know that's disgraceful! And you with 'principles' who touches no foreign letters!"

"Let us not get agitated, Herr Director General. Such agitation can only hurt, and I'm not a friend of dramatic scenes outside the stage. You yourself must see the damage it could do. This impulse that made you try to grab the revolver was one of weakness, which was definitely unworthy of you. Just don't lose your calm. You are one of the great thieves that one lets go—must let go, unfortunately. You do believe me that I honestly regret that?"

"Go on, let's get to the end!"

"I'm already doing it. First, I wanted to tell you just two more things. First of all, that you would have long been behind bars as a result of my efforts, if the interests of the ABB didn't require your knavery. You don't mind that at this stage, I make no bones about it? It's nothing to be shouted from the rooftops, but, of course, that isn't ruled out if our negotiations don't lead to the desired goal. And secondly, one has one's principles, and I will, in fact, never actually do something unlawful or even improper. But it is neither unlawful nor improper for the employer to search through the affairs of a disloyal employee, my dear Herr Director General! The president was present during the search."

"Finish!"

"I didn't find much. The fact that you would rather keep the evidence of your despicable romantic adventures in your office than in the vicinity of your wife, is understandable, but does not concern us. So, not much, but still two valuable clues. First, the aforementioned address, and second, the proof of your connection with the National Bank under the alias of your mother-in-law."

"It isn't an alias. The money really belongs to her!"

"It would be bad for us if it were so, but it isn't. You see, Herr Director General, without wanting to, you helped me have a career that I didn't want myself. First, I had to become a board member, and then it was absolutely necessary that I become a censor of the National Bank. With the mighty help of our president, that went smoothly. I had to do this in order to get a very accurate insight. So, you cannot now tell me a taradiddle about your mother-in-law. After all, I will, even today, become Director General, but only until we have found a suitable substitute for you."

"You continue to act as if I had committed fraud. You have yet to offer me proof!"

"But, dear Herr Director General (it's probably the last time I'll call you that), do you still not understand your situation? I can tell you in a few words how you did it. You knew Benk from an earlier date, and knew that it was the yearning of his life to create a sphere of influence in America, in the atmosphere of freedom. When he had closed the books and was about to go on holiday, you offered him sixty thousand crowns to disappear without a trace. No blemish could fall on his name, since he had delivered the cash box in full order and had his receipt in his pocket. His disappearance would indeed cause consternation, but otherwise no disadvantage whatsoever. For you, the consternation would be of immeasurable advantage to secure your position. After all, you were the only one who could ensure that the organization proceeded undisturbed, and thus your indispensability would be strikingly documented. To you, this was worth the sacrifice of Benk's reputation. Benk was persuaded, all the more so as you knew him from school. You spoke to one another in an informal manner, only, of course, not at the bank, at your request."

"It simply didn't work—because of the other employees."

"I understand. Now you could risk the big coup. You felt safe. The suspicion would fall on the missing cashier. You could know, or at least assume with good reason, that no one would report the loss to the authorities for fear of the public scandal. By the way, you had also taken steps for this eventuality. Shall I recap them for you?"

"Thank you, no need."

"Well, I will only point out that I have also unearthed a few things at, among others, HAPAG, the Hamburg-American Parcel Boat Stock Company. I wrote down the number of the cabin you rented on the *Kolumbia*. The holiday would have given you sufficient time to gain the desirable lead."

"What do you want from me now?"

"A trifle, your signature. You have power of attorney over the deposit of your 'mother-in-law' at the National Bank. The deposit is just enough to cover the ABB's damages. You will transfer this authority to me. Here is the fully prepared document. You need only place your worthy name underneath."

"I will not do that!"

"You understand, it isn't necessary. I want what's best for you. Only when you have convinced yourself, should you sign, otherwise not. The circumstances have indeed shifted to your disadvantage, sir. All precautions for safeguarding this deposit have been made in case of your refusal. You must understand perfectly clearly that the ABB now no longer has any cause to avoid taking legal action. The possible bad impression of the news of the great embezzlement would be counteracted by the fact that, not only has its author been promptly caught, but also immediate reparation has been promptly provided for. Now, what do you think?"

The Director General signed. Dagobert dispatched

the document with a trustworthy man who waited in the anteroom.

"Only two more minutes," he resumed. "The National Bank is right next door. In the meantime, I can tell you that it will be an apt surprise for our president, an innocent joy that he didn't expect. For I have not told him or anyone else of the progress of my efforts. I love coming back with finished facts. One has one's peculiarities!"

After a few minutes, a signal from the telephone resounded on the desk. The Director General put the receiver to his ear.

"The National Bank," he announced, "I don't understand. 'The Moor can go—the end!'"

"That's right," cried Dagobert. "That's the password I set up to confirm that everything was all right. And now, Mr. Ringhoff, you are the former Director General! Allow me to open the doors. The monitoring has now been lifted."

Ringhoff took his hat, bowed, and left the ABB, never to enter again.

Anonymous Letters

For some time, Andreas Grumbach, the president of the Industrialists Club, had been troubled by frequently recurring anonymous letters, which, however, served their purpose only to a very imperfect degree. Andreas Grumbach, because of his wealth, his prestige in business circles, and his social position, was among the greats of this world, and these cannot be easily intimidated by letters. If one receives and flies through one hundred or more letters every day, one soon becomes really rather indifferent, and many a sender would be very disappointed in his expectations and hopes, if he saw for himself how little the moral effect penetrated, which he intended to achieve with his letter. There is no longer any trace of those emotions, which someone who receives a letter once in a blue moon feels at the sight of a postman.

By and by, Andreas Grumbach began to recognize the letters. It was always the same peculiar paper, and they always showed the odd perpendicular handwriting, and now he always threw it unopened in the wastebasket. That would have been the end of the matter. But there was something that complicated the case a bit. Grumbach's wife was also positively besieged with this kind of letter and she didn't approach them with the same cool philosophy as her husband. She was unhappy, cried a lot, became nervous, and no longer dared to be among people. All persuasion was useless. She could not come out of her agitation at all, she didn't have a happy moment, and her life was almost destroyed.

Mrs. Grumbach, too, held a prominent position in society, and she was more anxious about it than would have been strictly necessary, for no one thought of disputing or undermining it. But there was still a feeling of insecurity in her. She was the minor actress Violet Moorlank when Grumbach took her for his wife. Hence the uncertainty. It was true that wicked talk had never come to her, but the secret fear that society would not recognize her and take her seriously she had never quite got rid of. This anxiety was now quite unfounded, for her husband's reputation was stable and strong enough to make her position unquestionable. But this fear once aroused, was never completely quelled, and was now, of course, greatly increased by those terrible letters, with their treacherous, malicious, and unspeakably vulgar contents.

At this point Andreas Grumbach decided to do everything in his power to put an end to the matter. He had, in fact, his friend Dagobert Trostler, the long-time man-about-town, whose great passion it was to amuse himself as an amateur investigator in his ample leisure time. Trostler had already provided him with essential services in some difficult and delicate cases with his ingenuity and art of synthesis; he would surely be able to offer advice, in this case, too.

Dagobert was a family friend of the Grumbach's, and

when the three of them were sitting at the table again, Grumbach explained the case by first speaking only about those letters which had been sent to him.

"So that's it, Frau Violet!" replied Dagobert, turning to the housewife. "Do you know, my most gracious lady, that I am seriously angry with you? You have a tribulation and keep it secret from me. You don't breathe a word. Is that how it should be?"

"Who said anything about me?"

"We're talking only about you. Your husband is a man and a man easily ignores certain disreputable behaviour. But I should have a bad understanding of the psychology of those anonymous beasts if I believed that they contented themselves only with torturing the man when there was such a beautiful opportunity to mistreat the woman, too. That is still always the more rewarding and safe enterprise."

"Dagobert, one really cannot keep anything secret from you," replied Violet. "Well, all right, yes. I am abused with these terrible letters, and they will drive me to despair."

"It was not difficult for me, according to your husband's hints, to understand the source of your grief. I knew there was a sorrow, and I have long seen it in you. But as you kept silent, I couldn't ask. Will you show me the letters? "

"Not for the world!"

"I understand. They are too disgusting, but ultimately, it will be necessary, if we are to discover the perpetrator, be it a man or a woman."

"A woman? No woman writes like that!"

"Let us beware of preconceived opinions. You know my views, Frau Violet. In all that is good and great, I place woman higher than man; in all that is evil, or rather, malicious, I place her lower. In any case, give me the letters, all those you have in your possession. Grumbach has thrown his away. That was hasty and is very unfortunate. The more material I have, the more I can hope to discover a clue."

Frau Violet brought the letters, a whole stack, probably sixty or eighty.

"But you must not read them in my presence," protested Frau Violet. "I would sink into the earth with shame."

"I'll study them at home," Dagobert reassured her. "First, let us examine only a few externalities here. The letters are all perfectly the same in shape. Reseda green paper with pretensions to elegance, yet at the same time only a cheap and bad imitation of the dignified, crafted Dutch handmade paper—unfortunately!"

"Why, 'unfortunately,' Dagobert?"

"Because I had secretly already harbored certain hopes. In fact, I already had a case involving anonymous letters. But it was easy as pie. This one seems much more difficult."

"What sort of case was that? You must tell me, Dagobert!"

"With pleasure, my dearest, but for the time being, let's stay with this matter. Everything indicates that the sender—he or she—works with great caution. Indeed, the handwriting does not allow one to draw a conclusion as to the sex. I can say that, because of all there is to learn in terms of graphology through study and observation, I have made a real effort to learn."

Dagobert examined the addresses with a pocket magnifying glass and then thought hard. At the same time, he twisted the tuft of hair on his little St. Peter's parting so that it soon stood up like a lock of clown's hair.

"There is such a muddle of masculine and feminine here that one could become positively crazy," he said to himself. "This is either a very masculine woman or a feminine man. Have you really no suspects, Frau Violet?"

"Not the slightest idea!"

"We cannot place any special hopes on graphology here. When the handwriting is disguised—and here it is disguised systematically and with consistency—graphology must fail. Here, we can only suppose that the hand that wrote this usually writes a slanting script. That's all. Because of the steep upright position here, the characteristics of the handwriting are, of course, completely altered, and the question is very much whether the letters will give me enough clues to reconstruct the original character."

"So, you have no hope, Dagobert, of exposing the villain?"

"The case interests me, and I will make every effort. Above all, I have to study the material. It may be possible that clues can be found in the contents of the letters, from the style, from individual phrases, from the orthography. Before that, there isn't much to say. How cautiously it has been worked, for example, you can see from the postmarks. As you can see, almost every letter carries a different postmark. This one, post office 66, this one post office 125, here post office 13, 47, 59. The letters were posted on long walks or drives. It is, of course, impossible to monitor a particular post office or mailbox."

"So, you really have no hope?"

"I said I will make every effort, so I'm hopeful."

"That sounds quite confident, Dagobert."

"Ultimately, one must dare!"

"You said you had already had a similar case, Dagobert. How was that?" Frau Violet was understandably very curious to learn more about this.

"The case, as I mentioned, was very simple, but it still gave me much pleasure. One day the adjutant of Archduke Othmar appeared, and summoned me to the Archduke's palace. So, I go with him immediately, and, in a private audience, the Archduke gives me the flattering disclosure that he has heard with particular interest some of my achievements as an amateur detective. He, too, now has an assignment, or rather a request. Of course I immediately made myself available, and remarked that His Imperial Highness had only to command.

"The case was like yours. It was anonymous letters, and here, too, not only the master of the house, but also his most illustrious wife had been sent them. The Archduke told me that he had a great deal of interest in finding out the writer, but that he was reluctant to turn to the police. After all he had heard, he had more confidence in me in this matter.

"Fine. I had the letters given to me. It was amazing. There were hundreds of them! I took them with me."

"Were they very cruel?" asked Frau Violet curiously.

"Oh, my dearest, whatever may have been written to you, it is impossible that the vulgarity and cruelty laid on in those has been reached, let alone surpassed."

"And you solved this knotty problem?"

"I was lucky. The thing was done in twenty-four hours."

"Tell me, Dagobert!"

When I took the letters, my first question was, of course, whether the authorities had any suspects or clues. The question was answered in the negative. So, I took the letters home with me, read them carefully and then reflected for a good two hours, but without coming to any significant result. The first half-day passed without a half-rational idea having occurred to me. It was not until night when enlightenment came, literally as I slept. I had gone to bed, and after long, fruitless efforts to fall asleep, at last the first slumber had come upon me, from which, however, I soon awoke, as if in alarm. Now, suddenly, there was an idea that could be built on. The letters lay on my nightstand. A fine chypre scent had reached my nose from them. Chypre is a distinctive perfume. I put on the lights, as much light as was at all possible, and picked up the letters again. One thing immediately became clear to me: the initial intensive study of the writing and the contents of the letters had been completely superfluous and useless. I had to stick only to externalities and could work only from those. In spite of the baseness of the contents, a certain noble atmosphere surrounded the letters. Certainly, a deliberate intention to deceive and misdirect was there as well, but even so—it pointed to a distinguished house, if not to noble origin altogether. A treacherous lackey or a malicious maid might have had a hand in the game. They could have taken the perfumed paper from their masters. Of the perfume I could hope, however, for no explanation, but—the paper! I am expert in paper varieties. It was the most exquisite and, I may say, the most precious luxury paper I had ever held in my hands. It was therefore a rather expensive luxury to send such letters *en masse* into the world, and if the sender didn't steal the paper, then he must certainly be in a position to enjoy this luxury.

Early in the morning, I took my carriage and visited some of the best stationery shops. I laid a torn, unmarked page of a letter in front of me and ordered that sort. From the outset, I had been prepared for the information I received. They didn't keep this variety: it was too expensive and would probably not sell. The information pleased me. This made the circle significantly smaller for my research.

Now I entered the store L. Wiegand, Court Supplier, on Am Graben Street with some excitement. I knew that this business was undoubtedly the most distinguished of the city. I showed the pattern, and the proprietor, who personally served me, immediately presented me with the desired highly elegant box with a hundred sheets and the corresponding envelopes. Sixty crowns! I bought it, but asked for a private interview.

The man led me into the small office behind his shop.

"I would like to know from you, Mr. Wiegand," I began, "whether this paper is also sold in another shop in Vienna."

"Certainly not," he replied self-assuredly. "The source of supply is my secret."

"It is an English product," I said, to flaunt my expertise a little.

"Indeed, but there is only one factory that produces it. This isn't an item for other shops," he added contemptuously. "It would be left lying there."

"Do you sell a lot of it?"

"Oh, a great deal, I'm happy to say."

I saw that I had not quite tackled the interview correctly. If I let him continue boasting, I would deviate further and further from my goal. So, I took a dozen letters out of my pocket to legitimize myself to a certain extent, and showed him the inscriptions. The effect was a satisfactory one. His face immediately took on an expression of reverence.

"Mr. Wiegand," I said, "you are a supplier to the Court and surely you must be anxious to do your duty to the Court."

He bowed very devoutly, and laid his hand on his heart to indicate that—for the Court! —he was ready to give his life.

"So, Mr. Wiegand," I went on, "Their Most Supreme Sovereigns will owe you thanks, if you answer some questions. Do you really sell much of the paper?"

"Sir, I do my business with it, along with the rest. Of course, I could not live from that alone."

"I can imagine. Are you in a position to name the main customers for this item? Please note well, Mr. Wiegand, the precise answer to this question is of special importance to Their Imperial Highnesses!"

The man was all willingness and devotion. He positively buckled whenever I mentioned the High Ruler. He reflected and then confessed that he had only three clients for this paper. He supplied the paper to the Serbian Court, then there was Lady Primrose from the English Embassy, but the biggest customer was Countess Tildi Leys, who appeared at least once a month to buy a box.

"Thank you, Mr. Wiegand. I will not fail to mention your kind assistance in high places."

Then I went. I was satisfied. For now the circle had

already drawn much smaller. So, three starting points and all three actually of equal value. I had to assess them. For I have made it my principle, in my profession, to regard from the very beginning nothing at all as improbable unless I have good reasons for such an assumption.

To begin was doubtless with Countess Leys. Not only because the investigation seemed to be the easiest and most comfortable, but because there was already definite, promising information at hand. The heavy consumption was, after all, conspicuous.

I looked at the clock: ten o'clock. From the postmarks of the letters, I had discovered that they had been posted almost without exception at the same time, around twelve o'clock in the afternoon, but at different places.

I directed my carriage into Reisnerstrasse and stopped opposite the Palais Leys, and there I remained leaning back in my carriage in observation. In my line, one must be patient. I didn't let myself become irritable, and I kept a keen eye on who came out of the house. The domestic staff didn't interest me. For two things had already become clear to me: first, that the letters had not come from the staff. If the Countess used only about one box per month—which was, of course, a great deal under normal circumstances—it was impossible for enough paper to be stolen for all those letters without her noticing. And secondly, if you write such letters, you don't consign the task to the servants. One deals with such a thing oneself, and highly privately.

I had waited about an hour, when a pompous porter came out of the palace gate to safeguard the exit of an equipage. I gave my coachman a sign. We followed the carriage.

As long as we drove, I remained sitting calmly. Nothing could happen. But when, after about a half-hour's drive, the equipage stopped, I quickly jumped out of my carriage. We were on the Schottenring, and the most beautiful spring sunshine lit the scenery.

A quick glance informed me that a mailbox was nearby. From the equipage, supported by a servant, an elegant young lady of quite extraordinary beauty, blond, with a pure Madonna's face, emerged. She walked toward the mailbox. I was there quicker, opened the flap, and held it as if I wanted to be helpful and let her go ahead. She thanked me with a slight inclination of her head and an engaging smile. Then, when she tried to push her letter into the gap, I snatched it from her fingers with a swift grab and put it safely into my pocket.

She looked at me, aghast and as if paralyzed. She didn't say a word at first, and was close to fainting.

"Forgive me, Countess," I said, "it had to be so!"

Only now did she find words again.

"Who are you? What do you want? You have committed an infamy. Give me my letter back, or I shall call for police assistance."

"That would be the best thing you could do. Countess. I would like to point out that we are standing just outside the police station, so if you'd like, I have a few more letters here that we could consult for comparison."

I pulled out a little packet of letters from my pocket and showed it to her. She became very pale and was now close to losing her composure completely. The servant, who only now seemed to notice that everything was not quite right, approached to offer his protection.

"Above all, Countess, keep that rascal at arm's length. He does not need to hear what we are discussing."

One glance from her commanded the servant back.

"And now, Countess, allow me to explain. My name is Dagobert Trostler. I am no official, which may reassure you, but I am commissioned by Their Highnesses to put an end to an ugly phantom. You have written your last such letter."

She nodded silently, and as she stood there so completely destroyed, I began to feel sorry for her. What can I say? One has one's weaknesses, and I have never been able to stand up properly against a woman's beauty. Yes, she was a very guilty woman, but she was lovely. "We cannot just keep standing here," I continued. "Do you want to take me with you in your carriage, or do you prefer to promenade with me and let our carriages go on ahead?"

She preferred the latter, and so we walked intimately side by side.

"What will you do now, Mr. Trostler?" she asked.

"What I must, Countess. I will report to my high clients."

"You will name me?"

"I must."

"Then you will have pronounced a death sentence."

"A social death sentence, perhaps. It would not be undeserved."

"Not only socially. If you do this, then today is my last day alive."

I looked at her. This was not spoken rhetorically. There was something glimmering in her eyes that indicated an unwavering resolution. Well, you know, Frau Violet, one is ultimately not a monster. It was a disgraceful, an ugly crime that had been committed. This ideal girl-beauty had been writing down words every day that would make a sergeant blush for his dragoons, but a suicide—I would not have liked to have that on my conscience.

"You didn't let her go without a penalty, Herr Dagobert?" cried Frau Violet, with barely disguised indignation.

"No. Punishment is necessary. I was only hesitant whether it had to be the death penalty. In my memory I had some notes about the noble family Leys. The young lady's father had been an alcoholic and died in delirium. A brother was an epileptic. No doubt there was a hereditary burden, which alone was to explain the perverse tendency for this young woman to write such shameful things."

"Hereditary burden!" cried Frau Violet, in annoyance. "This is the usual excuse. No, tell me honestly, Dagobert. You looked for extenuating circumstances!"

"Not extenuating circumstances, merely the psychological explanation for what seems to be completely incongruous. Let me be brief. After talking back and forth for some time, I didn't give a firm promise, but I agreed to try not to reveal her name if it was halfway possible. Then she took a little golden tin from her reticule, opened it, and showed me its contents. They were considerable chunks of cyanide. I know it by sight. That was enough to destroy a whole family, root and branch. She said, not at all pathetically, but convincingly, that she would free herself from life that same day if I made her name known.

"I took the little tin from her hand the better to admire the wonderfully delicate work. It was a masterpiece of baroque style craftwork. Of course, I didn't give it back to her. I made a pact with her. I would certainly drop in on her later today and then return to her the tin together with its contents. In turn, she would promise not to commit any hasty action until then, and to give up the suicide idea, if I could manage to bring the whole affair to a close without betraying her name."

"Did you not promise her a special reward for her fine performance?" asked Frau Violet, really quite displeased.

"On the contrary, I dictated a punishment to her. Our pact was very clear. I love clarity in all arrangements. If I didn't manage to keep her name secret, then, *vogue la galère*, she was free to do what she thought best. But if I were able to serve her, she would have to pay penance."

"What penance?" asked Frau Violet.

I believe I was strict enough. The solemn promise of never again doing such a thing, of course, I don't consider penance. That was self-evident. I therefore demanded either two years' in a convent or a five-year banishment from Vienna, to begin immediately. She chose the latter. We parted with a very friendly handshake.

I now went to the palace of the Archduke, and was immediately admitted, although the High Rulers were sitting at luncheon, and I was not dressed completely according to etiquette. The Archducal Couple were lunching alone. At a nod from the High Lady, a place was laid for me, and I doughtily kept pace. My expedition had given me an appetite.

As long as the attending servant came and went, no mention was made of the matter that had led me there. Only once the table was cleared and the air was pure did His Imperial Highness speak of our business.

"Now, my dear Herr Dagobert," the Archduke began, smiling—please note, my dearest, he said

Dagobert, because he might have heard that I was only called that in my circle of friends. He thus wished to give me proof of his appreciation. "You have undoubtedly come to request more information. Unfortunately, we cannot help you with that."

"First, I only come as a messenger," I replied. I took the intercepted letter out of my pocket, and passed it reverentially to the Archduchess, to whom it was addressed.

You can imagine her expression was anything but gracious. She had already had enough of such letters.

"I ask Your Imperial Highness," I continued, 'to draw your closest attention to a circumstance: the letter bears no postmark!"

It was the Archduke who first began to see.

"Yes, but then—Herr Dagobert—then you must know the offender already! Or what else can this mean?"

"It means, Imperial Highness, that I have come to the bottom of the muddy spring, and have plugged it. This was the last of these letters and none will follow. In this case I was happily able to do without the service of the Post Office. I personally pledge that no continuation will follow."

"Thank you so much, Herr Dagobert!"

The Archduchess also thanked me, emotionally, and asked, "So, who is the sender?"

"A lady."

"A lady? That's incredible!"

"It is so, Highness—a lady of society."

The rulers had to compose themselves first to be able to believe it. Then, of course, they sought the name very eagerly.

First, I gave a report on the details of my inquiry, as far as I thought it advisable and admissible, in the given case, and one was not sparse with words of praise. After all, it can indeed be said that I am not free of vanity, but neither am I the man to hide his light under a bushel.

"As to the name," I concluded my report, "I would leave the decision as to whether or not I really should name her, to the wisdom and grace of Your Imperial Highnesses."

I described things as they were, and didn't conceal the fact that revealing the name would in all likelihood lead to a catastrophe.

The Archduke frowned. "Here, indeed, there is truly no occasion to be treated with special grace."

"I think so, too," Frau Violet interrupted the narrator. She was in a very punitive mood against the cowardly sender of anonymous letters, and she had indeed good reason to be so.

"However, I still advocate leniency," I continued, and I developed my reasons for it. I was convinced that the threat of suicide had not been an empty phrase. I emphasized the gold tin with the cyanide tablets as confirmation of my statement, and added that I had promised to return them today.

"You must not, Herr Dagobert!" cried the Archduke.

"I have promised it, Imperial Highness. And of course, if such a decision is firm, one knows how to do it even without such a tin. I will disclose the name, if Your Highnesses insist on it, but before this I would like only to point out a circumstance for your gracious discretion. Your Highnesses desired that the matter be settled in silence and without a furor. With a suicide, one can never know whether a letter might be left behind that could then lead to sensational and unpleasant consequences. I have presumed, with your kind permission, to punish the perpetrator with a five-year banishment from Vienna.

The Archduke agreed at once, and his rapid change of mind surprised me a little.

"'Actually, I believe," he said, with a glance at his wife, "that we must leave the judgment to the Archduchess here."

The Archduchess had thoughtfully looked at the deadly poison in the tin, which she had taken from my hand. Now she looked up and said, "It isn't my place to pronounce a death sentence."

Then she gave me back the tin, thanked me once

more with great warmth, and proffered her hand to kiss. As she pulled back, the Archduke secretly tapped me on the shoulder. I took this as a sign that I should still linger to receive a confidential message. I was not mistaken.

"One moment, Herr Dagobert," he said, when his wife had left the room. "I would like to tell you something else. I know the offender. Because I noticed with a glance what both you and my wife have overlooked. Virtually concealed among the intricate ornaments on the lid of the tin is a tiny coat of arms, which I recognize."

"I saw for myself and am ashamed. I completely missed that!"

"'And yet you were much wiser than I, Herr Dagobert. It is actually a very sad story. I loved this lady, and I may assume that she, too, had feelings for me. It may well be that it was love which turned into its ugliest distortion here, and it will be a good thing for the lady to be allowed a few years' leisure to think about her shameful aberration in her castles, or, for all I care, in London or Paris"

This, Frau Violet, is the story of my first case with anonymous letters.

"But did you see the Countess again, Dagobert?"

"Naturally. On the very same day, as I had promised."

"Well, and?"

"She was prepared, prepared for everything. She repented and took the punishment."

"A fine punishment—in castles or in Paris!"

"At all events, still a punishment, my dearest, which made possible contemplation and repentance, perhaps even complete reform."

"You would not ooze humanity so, dear friend, if perhaps she had been less handsome."

"Quite possibly. One should not dissemble," replied Dagobert, as he twisted the tuft of hair again. "In any case, I was and am completely satisfied with myself in this matter. The countess asked me to keep the small tin in memory of her and as a pledge of her reform. I was also to believe she would always remember me in unquenchable gratitude. I kept the treasure and incorporated it into my collection."

"It only strikes me now, Dagobert, that I have never heard of a noble family of Leys in my life."

"Yes, did you really believe, my dearest, that I would betray her true name to any person in the world? The name was, of course, invented."

"But the person is alive?"

"She lives and she has kept her promise so far. There is also little prospect that she'll return soon, or indeed ever. She now forms the distaff half of a couple abroad and is said to play a great role there."

"I am particularly interested," now spoke up Mr. Grumbach, who had hitherto listened silently, "how a well-educated, high-ranking young lady can come to such a terrible and dishonest aberration."

"Here we are again at the starting point," replied Dagobert. "I only told the whole story to show that we have to guard against preconceived opinions. 'No woman writes like that!' Frau Violet exclaimed in a categorical manner almost, brooking no contradiction. I have shown, however, that a woman and even a delicate girl certainly can write in this way, and even worse. I don't mean to say that these letters must also have come to you from a female hand, I merely wanted to advise caution, and to warn you against a hasty judgment."

"Now I understand," cried Frau Violet, "why you so regretted the shabby elegance of our letters, Dagobert."

"Very right, most gracious, as you see. It's not helpful. Ten or twenty thousand people write on this paper in Vienna. I can't run through all the stationery shops."

"But you will make the effort, Dagobert?"

"Certainly, most gracious, I will make every effort."

"You promise?"

"I promise it."

Dagobert took the letters with him, and he pointedly asked Grumbach that, if any more letters arrived—as was certainly to be expected—they should not be thrown into the wastebasket. They should be left unread by Grumbach. Frau Violet, too, had better not read them, but Dagobert must get them all in his hands. The more material, the better. The case was decidedly more difficult than the one he had been talking about, and it was now necessary to search for clues with all possible care. For this purpose, every single letter had to be thoroughly studied. Not one must remain unconsidered.

Frau Violet was really quite impatient. If anything, she gladly would have seen the secret revealed the very next day. Dagobert, however, placated her, and urged patience. He could not make a definite promise whether he would finally succeed in lifting the veil, but in any case, it would be weeks, if not months. Finally, to have peace, he forbade Frau Violet ever to speak of the matter. He himself would initiate the discussion if there were anything to be reported. Before then, talking about it would have no purpose, and could do no good.

Frau Violet dutifully maintained discipline. She no longer asked, but found it terribly hard. For she was very curious, and if, keeping the agreement faithfully, she didn't ask, she nevertheless directed many an anxious glance at Dagobert when they were sitting together after dinner in the smoking room in the usual manner, she at her favorite spot at the marble fireplace, Dagobert opposite her, and Grumbach on his comfortable armchair farther to the middle of the room.

After holding out bravely thus for several days, Dagobert let himself be moved by her longing eyes.

"It is a slow process, Frau Violet," he began, "but it's moving forward. We might have some tentative clues already."

"Have you really found out anything, Dagobert?" she asked in the most intense excitement.

"It is very little, but it is a point of departure, perhaps the Archimedean point."

"What kind of point?"

"Archimedean. One needs it to lift the world out of the hunt. You know, my dear, that Archimedes—"

"Yes, I know, but now no mythology, Dagobert!"

"Permit me to say, my dear, Archimedes does not belong—"

"Yes, but for my sake! Let's just leave the Archimandrites, or whatever they are called, alone. I will believe everything you say about them without hesitation, but now tell me what you have found out!"

"Some little things. So, the writer—I am quite sure now that it is a male writer and not a female writer—is smoothly shaved and smokes cigarettes. I believe you make a disappointed face, Madame? It is indeed very little, but one can build on it."

"You cannot possibly go through all the people, Dagobert, who are smooth-shaven and smoke cigarettes!"

"That would certainly be a little complicated, though perhaps not so much as you imagine, Frau Violet. The letter writer, it is proven, knows you very well. You see that we already have a circle with very specific limits. So, it would not be so complicated, it would just not be safe enough for me."

"So—why smooth-shaven?"

"It's just a guess, and no certainty yet. That is why I don't wish to comment on it now. I therefore ask for another eight days. Then I shall be able to tell you more, perhaps everything."

"And why a cigarette smoker?"

"That's a matter for discussion. Cigarette smoker alone, that would be too little for me as a point of reference. I am able to go somewhat further in my conclusions. It is someone who has the habit of smoking self-rolled cigarettes. There isn't much achieved with this either, but every circumstance is of value in drawing the circle smaller."

"How did you get to this, Dagobert?"

"In my business, one must be a stickler for detail. In two of the many letters, I found a tiny speck of tobacco, scarcely larger than a pin-tip, just as much as would hang on a pen stroke as the ink dried. In tobaccos, as you know, I am a connoisseur. I took the magnifying glass to confirm what I already knew, because I have good eyes. These were particles of Sultan Flor."

"And equipped with this knowledge, will you go out to catch the thief, Dagobert?"

"Sultan Flor is a long and fine-cut, light yellow Turkish tobacco. It is chiefly used for self-rolled cigarettes, but occasionally also smoked in a long-stemmed Turkish pipe. That is why I still have to reserve judgment on my original statement. It could also be a Turkish pipe smoker, although these are not nearly as numerous as the cigarette smokers. Sultan Flor is a very good tobacco, and it is particularly recommended to people who want to smoke decently yet cheaply."

"Yes, that reassures me tremendously," replied Frau Violet dryly, a little sensitive to the scantiness of the revelations she had received, but there was no more to be got out of Dagobert that day.

For the next eight days, Frau Violet, fortunately, didn't get around to occupying herself much with the unfortunate letter affair. She had her head full of other things, and her hands full. Two great soirées at the Grumbach house in one week! Dagobert had arranged them and hidden himself behind the figure of Grumbach. Frau Violet was not to know anything about his intention. He wanted to look comfortably around the whole circle of Grumbach acquaintances up close. There would have been too many people for one evening, so two were organized. A division was worked out. First came his friends, and then hers. To prepare and carry out two soirées, of course, Dagobert encountered no opposition from Frau Violet.

When the hustle and bustle was over, the three of them sat cozily together again in the smoking room one day, and Dagobert complimented the housewife on her two beautiful parties.

"They are the talk of the city," said he, "and opinion is unanimous in the admiration of your housewifely virtue, Frau Violet."

"Were you satisfied with me too, Dagobert?"

"I was simply delighted."

"That pleases me. Because I know you are a severe critic, Dagobert. But I cannot get rid of a suspicion. That is to say, the idea came to me afterwards that I actually had to do these soirées for you?"

"For me?"

"Yes, for study purposes. I feel as if you wanted to relate the whole events in some way to your investigations in the matter of the letters."

"I bow my head, my dearest: You've seen through me."

"Well, did it help, at least?"

"I rather think we have advanced a step. It is clear from the contents of the letters that their sender belongs to your acquaintances, perhaps even your most intimate acquaintances. I wanted to see them together all at once. I would have regarded it as a success if the result had been a purely negative one, and I had gained the conviction that the writer was not to be found in your narrow circle."

"It would be very welcome to me, Dagobert, if you had come to this conclusion, and I would not have minded at all if my efforts had been in vain."

"Then I would have to reproach myself for having caused you the effort."

"Did you really find something, Dagobert?"

"I've reinforced an opinion, and that's something. I have my clue, and I believe it is the right one."

"Dagobert, it would be great if you could render us this service! Tell us whom you suspect."

"Not so fast, my dearest. Conjectures don't help us. We must have proof."

"Do not torment me like that, Dagobert! You know something. Say it!"

"It's no good to speak prematurely. I presume, my dear, that you, of course, have not spoken to anyone about this ugly affair."

"Of course not. That is, I have poured out my heart to one person, but it is the same as if I had not told anyone. Walter Frankenburg—"

"Walter Frankenburg!"

"My oldest friend from the stage, and he was already, back then, a truly paternal friend to me. When I married, he was my witness before the altar. This is a man whom I may tell everything."

"I have observed you, my dearest, when you've talked to him, and I would not have made my remark before, if I had not expected you to confide in him."

"You cannot blame me for it. The man is reliable."

"I would have thought it better not to speak at all. Did you tell him that you had entrusted me with the investigation?"

"You were not mentioned, Dagobert. I repeat that I would put my hand in the fire for Walter Frankenburg. He is a truly noble and honorable man. But let us leave that now. I would rather you told me more about your observations."

"So, we had two groups of guests, the Grumbach group and the Frau Violet group. I had little hope of the former from the outset. All the big industrialists and financial barons—they commonly have other worries than sitting down day after day and scribbling anonymous letters. Neither do they have, nor willingly take the time. The second group, the little party of artists, offered more prospect."

"Thank you for the compliment on behalf of the artists!"

"I didn't intend to hurt your feelings, Frau Violet. If you insist on it, I will even confirm that envy and resentment and spite are vices which are never present in the world of actors. That's the way I am!"

"I don't insist."

"Fine. I have previously mentioned to you that the letters were probably written by a smooth-shaven man. I didn't want to give the impression that I was capable of discovering this from the writing. The truth is that I have also studied the letters very closely for their stylistic expression. I noticed certain recurring phrases and expressions. They are, to cite a few examples, "it is to scream," "I gloat over," "a terrific part," "the talentless beast," "the advertising bugle." The examples are still piling up. Now, Frau Violet, don't you find a clue in them?"

"Certainly, Dagobert, when one is made aware!"

"I was, therefore, to suppose that a smooth-shaven gentleman was the author."

"Why a gentleman?"

"I remind you of the Sultan Flor."

"There are also ladies who smoke!"

"Absolutely, but they don't smoke chibouks, and they usually don't even roll their cigarettes themselves. So, I took a good look at the people with you, and when people took their leave I joined a group which seemed to offer me a few prospects."

"I certainly noticed it, Dagobert. Walter Frankenburg also joined you."

"He came along, too, and I am glad to confirm that he enjoys a high reputation in his circles. Outside of the stage, he is quite the *père noble*. We went on to a coffeehouse, as per the usual custom. Of course, your evening was discussed and thoroughly reviewed, Frau Violet."

"Was I judged very harshly?"

"Not in the least, I assure you. On the contrary. For a moment, however, I felt tempted to begin judging to encourage the others to continue."

"A good friend!"

"I didn't do it, although I could promise it would have met with success. A deep sediment of hatefulness must have accumulated in the writer, and when he was in society, something must come to light in artlessness. Be calm, Frau Violet. I didn't do it. One has one's principles, and even as *agent provocateur*, would not venture it even in the most extreme emergency."

"You should have done it even at that cost, Dagobert!"

"Not at all! Of course, we talked excellently. That was still on account of your splendid Rhine wine and Heidsieck, Frau Violet. I offered my best Havana and asked for a cigarette. Immediately a dozen tins were proffered to me. I declined. I now wished for a self-rolled cigarette to go with my little coffee. Only one person in the company could provide it. I took the tin—Sultan Flor!"

"Ah!"

"We got to talking. The man who had helped me told me a story, and he introduced it with the words, 'Children, it was a scream!' The story was quite crude, but the introduction had interested me. Then he came to speak about you, and he explained that Violet had a terrific success today."

"Who was it, Dagobert?"

"Let me continue to be careful, Frau Violet."

"But you seem to be really close to it now!"

"Perhaps even closer than you think, Frau Violet. I will be with you at an unusual time tomorrow, at ten o'clock in the morning, and if we don't attain our goal tomorrow, the next days at the same time. I beg you, Grumbach, to stay at home until I come. Your office will not run away in the meantime."

"And you don't want to say anything more now, Dagobert?"

"I cannot. Just one more thing: Should one of the letters again arrive, then please, hold the envelope obliquely against the light. I hope that you will discover a new nuance, because I believe that the ink will now display a metallic luster."

When Dagobert came back the next morning, he found Grumbach already eager to hold a newly received letter obliquely against the light. It was unmistakable: the ink had a metallic, green-gold luster. Frau Violet was in great excitement.

"Dagobert," she cried, "you are a sorcerer! How could you know?"

"Excuse me, my dear, for being a little unpunctual. I actually wanted to be here myself, when the messenger came. I know well enough now by which post these lovely letters tend to come, but you know full well I am an incorrigible late sleeper. It does not matter. Let's see. Right—the most beautiful metallic luster with which I have the honor, respectfully and devotedly—"

"What, Dagobert? You cannot mean to run away right now! First you must tell all."

"I must waste no time getting out the door, Frau Violet. There is still a lot to do. But I invite myself to dine with you today, and then I will tell you as much as you like."

He hurried away, and only appeared at five o'clock in the afternoon for dinner, as he had promised. He dined in comfort, while Frau Violet, in her excitement, left the delicious dishes almost untouched. She could hardly wait to hear his report, but she knew that he would not talk about the matter at the table, and she could not wish for it, because of the presence of the servants.

But when, after the meal, they had made themselves comfortable in the smoking room, Frau Violet, in her favorite spot, immediately gave Dagobert the floor.

"The work is done, Frau Violet," he began. "My mission is fulfilled. You will not be bothered with these miserable letters any longer. And you too, Grumbach, will be relieved of the inconvenience."

"As for me," replied the latter, "it would not have disturbed me very much in my routine. In any case, you have once again earned my deepest thanks, Dagobert."

"Tell me," urged Frau Violet.

"I don't know, my dear, whether it would not be more advisable for you to be satisfied with the liberation without delving into the details."

"Oh, no, Dagobert, I want to know everything!"

"Good. So, we have the wrongdoer."

"Who is it?"

"As I've already remarked, a smooth-shaven cigarette smoker. How I came to that, you know. We had got as far as one of your friends offering me from his bourgeois Sultan Flor."

"Who is it?"

"The next day I paid my visit to this man, at a time when I was sure that he would not be at home. I was able to know that, for I had inquired. He was, at that time, busy with a stage rehearsal. My visit was necessary and useful. I was able to make my arrangements. When I left you this morning, I went to the Criminal Commissioner Dr. Weinlich. His is the only capable mind in our criminal investigation department. We are friends and occasionally exchange experiences and observations. I can say, without being immodest, that we motivate each other and learn from one another. I presented him with the case, and asked him whether he would be so good as to protect the threatened honor and peace of a reputable house. I didn't ask for an official intervention, and even declared it to be out of the question. All I needed was an expert and impressive witness to the trial I had planned. He was on board instantly, and we went to see the man who this time—I had already assured myself of this—was at home. The coffee, by the way, is again excellent, Frau Violet, and as far as your brandy is concerned, I have long intended to ask—"

"Oh, Dagobert, let the brandy wait! Tell me more!"

"No really! About brandy, you must know, I am a

connoisseur, and there—"

"Oh!"

"All right, then, we found the man at home."

"Now, for the sake of God, tell us who he is!"

"He received us splendidly. At home as in public, entirely the *père noble*."

"Oh! You don't mean to say—"

"I do."

"But—not Walter!"

"Walter Frankenburg, the great mime and paternal philanthropist."

"That is terrible!"

He received us splendidly. He immediately tried to hug me, but I waved him off. I made it short and to the point. I introduced the Court chief police officer Weinlich, whom, I told Frankenburg, I brought with me, because we were on the trail of a very wicked, mean trick. Then I drew two letters out of my pocket, the one from the day before yesterday and today's, both still unopened.

"Do you know these letters, Mr. Frankenburg?"

"No. No one will believe—"

"What won't anyone believe?"

"That I wrote them!"

"Why wouldn't you have written them? Their contents could be highly respectable!

"He realized that he had trapped himself, and fell pale, but he remained ever the heroic father. This was his house and he would preserve the sanctity of his home. He was not disposed to be formally interrogated in his home because of a disgraceful as well as unfounded suspicion.

"I thought," I replied, "that you would prefer an interrogation here to the courtroom."

"In the courtroom, sir, you would be answerable!

"I am only afraid that you will not give me that opportunity. So, you deny it. That is your right. You don't, however, know that I hold you in an iron vice with my proof. You may fidget as much as you want, you cannot get out of this."

"I want to know the proof!"

"Immediately. I had the honor of stopping in on you yesterday. You did find my card?"

"Yes."

"Do you still have it?"

"Yes, here it is."

"Too bad. You should have destroyed it. For it paints a powerful, perhaps the strongest, piece of evidence against you."

"What can the card prove against me? You ask me on it whether I will perform in the Industrialists Club in the near future. So far, I have neither agreed nor refused. How am I supposed to have committed a crime?"

"You still don't want to admit anything. Let us, then, proceed methodically. First of all, it can be shown that the same stationery used for these anonymous scrawlings is present in your desk."

"Who can prove that?"

"I can. I was not sitting at this desk for five minutes in vain, albeit under the careful eyes of your secretary, who did me the honors. Here, Herr Detective Inspector, what perfume do these two letters have?"

"I believe it's a light violet perfume," replied Dr. Weinlich, after putting the letters to his nose.

"Whatever it is," I explained, "in any case, it's a cheap variety. I am an expert in perfumes. The main thing is, Herr Detective Inspector, will you sniff at the upper desk draw on the right?"

"It is, in fact, exactly the same perfume."

"This is the main thing. You'll refuse to unlock the drawer, Mr. Frankenburg. I don't need you to, although I believe we could find some evidence there. Not enough, though, I agree. You can be reassured. We don't have a home search warrant. We cannot force you to unlock it. We could, indeed, ultimately get such an order, but we don't need it. I have something better. When I had the privilege of sitting at this table, I used the opportunity to drip three drops of bronze ink dissolved in water into your inkwell from this locket ring that you see on my finger. You couldn't notice the little trick, Mr. Frankenburg, but it has caught you. The note I wrote was the last document written at this desk with lusterless ink. Everything written subsequently, once the ink has dried, shows the telltale and irrefutable metallic luster. Kindly compare these two letters, Herr Detective Inspector. One was written before, the other after my visit, as the postmarks show.

"This, too, is unmistakable," confirmed Dr. Weinlich.

"The fact is, you can have all the desks in Vienna searched legally, and on none of them will you find this extraordinary ink. Do you believe now, Mr. Walter Frankenburg, that I have caught you?"

"Well, did he confess?" Asked Frau Violet, in the most intense excitement.

"He was broken, gave up all resistance and told all. And now, Frau Violet, prepare yourself for the great trial!"

"What are you thinking, Dagobert? Should I perhaps stand as a witness, and be dragged through all the papers in the gossip columns?"

"Yes, what else should I do with the man?"

"Get him out of Vienna, give him a punishment, whatever you want, but leave me out of it."

"Strange how one can be deceived. I thought that because this kind of punishment seemed much too mild for the Countess—"

"Oh, that was quite different!"

"I don't know if it was different, but in any case, I banished him from the spot. He will never set foot on a Viennese stage again. In addition, he will send this amount to your charity, my dearest. He will see the announcement in the newspapers. The headline will be, 'From an unmasked villain,' and he will recognize himself."

An Arrest

At Grumbach's house they were sitting together in the smoking room over a little coffee. A small company: the host Andreas Grumbach, the meritorious president of the Industrialists Club, his charming wife Frau Violet, and the old faithful friend of the family Dagobert Trostler.

Today there was nothing new to tell. Dagobert had enjoyed a time of rest and recovery, which he had certainly deserved, for the last few weeks had been really quite exhausting, and had occupied his intellectual and physical powers very fully. First, he had, with extraordinary ingenuity, shed light on a dark crime of substitution of a child and the ensuing substantial property seizure, which had been committed almost sixty years ago. Soon after that, he had succeeded in getting to the bottom of a large-scale criminal stock market maneuver, through which all European exchanges were rocked, including even the International Commission, whose President Andreas Grumbach also was. It could have been disastrous. For these purposes, however, he had had to travel around almost all of Europe by carriage. It was no wonder, then, that he felt in need of a bit of rest afterwards.

A small dissatisfaction seized the housewife when the

two gentlemen disclosed that they wouldn't dine with her on the next Thursday—it would have been Dagobert's usual visiting day—since they had both received an invitation which could not be rejected.

Frau Violet pouted.

"I do not see," she replied, somewhat aggrieved, "why this should not be possible if one has obligations already. I could have expected from my husband that he would do the proper thing and not accept an invitation for himself alone."

"Dear child," the host hastened to soothe her, "I have otherwise always done the proper thing, but here it was an exceptional case. The invitation was expressly for a "gentlemen's evening.""

"Ahhh! Then yes, of course."

"Once again you harbor the blackest suspicion, Violet. Wrongly. The invitation is for a gentleman's evening—by day!"

"It's very unimportant to me whether the gentlemen wish to make night day or day night. That they— supposedly—wish to be among themselves. That is the decisive factor. With such piquant diversions, we have to stand back, of course. Of course, I understand perfectly!"

"Your suspicion is really unfounded, Violet. It is to be a very harmless garden party."

"Whatever it is—you had the very good excuse that you had a guest yourself, and so, too, did Dagobert, that he was already engaged. But I will of course immediately be pushed into the background when something 'better' is offered! Please, do not trouble yourselves, I won't hold you back."

"But most gracious Frau Violet," Dagobert now interposed, "it really could not be otherwise! Baron Weisbach has invited us. As you know, he is the vice-president of the International Commission, and he is vice-president of almost all the other companies headed by your husband. Andreas could therefore not refuse."

"My God, the freshly-baked Baron!"

"You should not speak contemptuously of him, Frau Violet. He deserves our respect. He wrote me a pretty word on my congratulations. Other aristocrats are proud of their old nobility, I of my young nobility."

"How did he actually come to be 'elevated' to the nobility?" asked Frau Violet, now half propitiated.

"It was actually very nice. In Vienna, as perhaps in all major cities, there is a need for public hospitals, in particular children's hospitals. One fine day, Mr. Weisbach—then, simply Mr. Weisbach, but not for long—reached into his pocket and dedicated one million to the construction of a children's hospital. But when it stood erect and equipped according to the latest regulations and achievements of science and humanity, Mrs. Weisbach, his wife, for her part, reached her hand into her pocket and also dedicated one million to its permanent preservation and operation. The Emperor too appeared at the opening ceremony with his retinue eight days ago. When the founder and his wife were introduced to him, he said: 'Baron Weisbach, I declare my unreserved appreciation to you, and to you, Baroness, my thanks for your generous deed.' And so, the ennoblement was complete. In Austria perhaps the first case of ennoblement on the spot."

Frau Violet found it all very nice, both Weisbach and the Emperor. She was also quite comforted about the other thing, but she made one more exception.

"I admit," she said, "that André could not easily refuse, but you, Dagobert, could have extricated yourself quite well. You were already invited!"

"I too could not free myself, my dear. For in fact I am a little to blame for everything."

"Why should you be to blame?"

"For everything, for the hospital foundation, and for the barony, and so on. But you, Frau Violet, are actually to blame for everything!"

"How could I be?"

"Very easily. You know very well, Frau Violet, that on your behalf, I must fence every moment for your charitable associations."

"Oh, if that is a burden to you, Dagobert—"

"I beg you—I am not complaining. I am merely establishing a fact. My first approach was always to Weisbach. There I was always sure to get something. Usually one thousand crowns, sometimes even ten thousand. Once we even pressed him for twenty thousand crowns. At the same time, however, I never looked as enthusiastic as he probably may have wished. Once he also made a sharp remark to me about whether it was so self-evident that he would throw money at me. I replied that this was not at all so self-evident, but very nice and praiseworthy of him, but in general I had to say that our wealthy people lacked the right impetus and great pull in their acts of charity. He didn't say anything to that and just looked at me like someone who really has nothing to say. We didn't talk about this point again. At the opening eight days ago, however, he took me aside, and asked with unmistakable inner satisfaction in his eyes whether this was enough 'impetus' and 'pull' for me."

Frau Violet now saw that Dagobert, too, could not send any refusal, and found in this, as she jestingly remarked, that she should mourn her youth alone this Thursday. Dagobert also jokingly replied with one of his twelve standing jokes: "Lunch is therefore not served to you, my dearest. What for? Nobody gives me anything either. So I will eat my part, if it's all right, a day later, on Friday."

Frau Violet was very much in favor. She went even further; she made a last advance to at least save some of her Thursday: "My husband said that the gentlemen's evening was to be held in the day. Thus, the evening might still be free. I do not want to be a spoilsport and do not want to push, but if it's not be too late, the gentlemen could still accompany me for a cup of tea. I'll wait gladly till ten o'clock."

"That is a brilliant idea, my dear!" exclaimed Dagobert enthusiastically. "After a sharp combat, and it may well become one, I still like to drink a cup of tea, and I can get none better than with you, Frau Violet. Also, it will not be as late as you think. On the invitation it's clearly "10-6 o'clock." Clear delineations are always pleasant. Thus, we will be able to take our tea at seven o'clock with you, and take that time to gossip a little."

***

And so it was. On Thursday evening—it was not even quite seven o'clock—the two gentlemen reported to Frau Violet and ebulliently claimed their rights to her cup of tea. They were in very good form, especially Mr. Grumbach, who never stopped laughing. Quite unlike his otherwise serious and dignified practice, he made plentiful and indiscriminate "jokes," which must have been very good, otherwise he wouldn't have been able to laugh so loudly and so heartily over them.

The tea was soon procured, and now they were sitting happily together in the smoking room. Frau Violet was already dreadfully curious, and of course, her first question was "Well, how was it?"

"Oh, it was great," said the host, who now took the floor. It was amazing how talkative he had become. "It was to be foreseen that Weisbach—ah, a thousand pardons! —Baron Weisbach—one will have to get used to that—an elegant twist—eh?"

He seemed to like "elegant twist" exceptionally well. He couldn't stop laughing at it.

"The restriction ten to six was expedient," said Dagobert quietly and with a side glance at Frau Violet, while Grumbach blustered on in his noisy laughter, "good wine makes you happy!"

"So, Baron Weisbach," Grumbach resumed, "hahahaha—very well—where was I, and what was I going to say?"

"That Baron Weisbach wouldn't shell out!" helped Dagobert, who was able to tolerate much more drink than his dear friend.

"Right—very good—that was it! So, everything wonderful, fine, in great style, *seigneurial*—well put, eh? —The man knows how to live and receive guests. And we entertained ourselves—famously! I still have to laugh." And he laughed. "The best thing was—you should have been there, Violet—how Dagobert was so convincing with his detective knowledge, and he lost face when Herr Chief Inspector Weinlich appeared and made a brilliant catch, and Dagobert sat there, the picture of misery. A European has rarely been so embarrassed."

Grumbach shook with laughter remembering it. Frau Violet, however, opened her eyes wide. "What? There had been something criminal, too? It's remarkable that where Dagobert goes, something is going on." She was very anxious to learn more, but she had no particular confidence in her husband's narrative skill, especially in his current state of merriment. She therefore turned to Dagobert for him to tell.

"He will not wish to tell you much, Violet," interrupted Grumbach, "for this time he has been miserably taken in. He contrived something, and

Weinlich was to fall for it. But he was not fooled, but rather nabbed the right one right off. You should have seen Dagobert's face. It was too delicious!"

"Is it true, Dagobert," asked Frau Violet. "Did you have bad luck for once?"

"On the contrary, my dear. I had good luck. Without a little luck, my profession doesn't work at all."

"And yet it was a failure?"

"Who says that?"

"My husband just said—"

"Him!" Dagobert gave the merry host a pitying look. "My God, he doesn't understand what happened at all, poor thing!"

"So tell me."

"Yes, he should tell it," the host agreed. "I am curious how he will scramble out of this!"

Dagobert, with quiet contempt, passed over this insinuation, and began to speak by directing his address to the housewife, and only to her. That was Grumbach's punishment.

"Baron Weisbach, as you may know, Frau Violet, had a magnificent villa built in Sievering. It is among the great attractions of Vienna. The background is formed by the heights of the Viennese forest, and, looking at that, you might think you were in a quiet remote forest, many miles away from the noise of the world's hubbub. Turn halfway around, and you can see the glittering Danube river and the million-strong city spread out at one's feet in shimmering splendor. The villa was built by Otto Wagner, so at first sight, a little crazy, but in truth, with a down-to-earth consideration of all relevant needs and every conceivable comfort. Otto Wagner's mode of art differs from other customary architectural styles to date—will you allow me, my dear, to explain it to you?"

"No, Dagobert, I will not allow that. Aesthetics and art criticism come later. As for me, I will keep still then, but for now, you must stick to the story line."

"Good. As an aesthetician, I have always been underestimated. I am already accustomed to this unjust treatment. May I yet remark, however, that the villa has, of course, a well-kept garden and a splendid park?"

"Yes, Dagobert, you may."

"Thank you. Indeed, this forms part of the story. So Weisbach had invited us for two reasons. First of all, for the inauguration of the new villa, and secondly, to give thanks for our congratulations. We were fourteen men at the most, his most intimate friends, who were to rejoice with him on the favor bestowed by the Emperor."

"And why only gentlemen?" asked Frau Violet, whose slight irritation on the point had not quite been overcome.

"Because there was only one gentleman, he himself, in the house. His wife, his sons, and his daughters had all gone to the North Sea, to Paris, to Switzerland."

"But you should have told me that immediately!"

"Yes indeed, Grumbach, you should have said at once!" agreed Dagobert, thus comradely turning all blame onto his friend's shoulders. "Breakfast was scheduled for ten o'clock, but we were all there a little earlier, and Weisbach began to show us the house. He acted as guide and led the company. I stayed a little behind, as I had seen it all repeatedly. From the staircase, as the last of the group, I casually threw a glance through a peephole window into the hall on the ground floor, where our overcoats hung. It seemed to me as if I had perceived a white glow in the half-dark. I had to deal with this first. An arm, a hand, the bright glimmer—someone had stolen a silver cigarette case from one of our overcoats."

"Stop, there I've caught him, Violet," Grumbach called with particular satisfaction. "Do not believe him! He told us the story quite differently. He told us that he had stolen the case himself, to set up a trap for Doctor Weinlich."

"I had my reasons. You will see, my dear, whether I have done right. So, I quietly let the company go up the stairs and ran around the house, in order to be able to meet my interesting character from the other side without any suspicion."

"And did you succeed?" asked Frau Violet.

"As I wished. Except, Weisbach himself almost put a spoke in my wheel. He had seen me from a window on the first floor, and called me just as I saw my man approaching me. Weisbach was very urgent: I was to go up at once. There was something there I had not seen. I was obliged to follow the call, whether I liked it or not, but first I took a good look at my man, who was of great interest to me. To my reassurance, his whole attire at once made me recognize that he belonged to the house. So I went out, confident that I would find him later."

"Yes, but a beautiful opportunity would have been missed," said Frau Violet, "since he might no longer have had the case with him."

"That is very true, Frau Violet. As I perceive, at all events, that you show far more talent for the noble detective art than your highly esteemed consort. Now, however, I didn't have the slightest interest in the case since I was already occupied with other, more important things. So, I went upstairs. What Weisbach wanted to show me was a watercolor by Rudolf Alt, a veritable masterpiece, which the aged master had only painted a few weeks before his death. As regards the peculiarity of the Alt technique—"

"We have agreed, Dagobert: the art criticism comes later!"

"Right. So I got to chatting with Weisbach, and I learned how splendid the picture was, and what it had cost. I let that pass over me and then directed the conversation as I wanted it. Had he seen the man who had just encountered me downstairs.

"'Oh, that is my gardener—a splendid man!'"

"'Why a splendid man?'"

"'In every respect. Firstly, he understands his business on the grounds. If you care to look at my garden, the greenhouses, and the park, you will already know what a pearl it is.'"

"'I've already seen that for myself partly—and what else?'"

"'The main thing: faithful like gold! The villa is indeed a little remote and lonely. My whole family is gone. I'm alone in the house. I was never a great hero. The uncertainty in the villas around Vienna is proverbial. So alone in the mansion by night, I could not close an eye, and therefore, since I have been alone in the mansion, I let Trautwein the gardener sleep in my room. Since then, I have slept like a king. This is indeed a reassuring protection. Just take a look, when you go down, at his hands. If a burglar ever gets into his hands, he will have nothing to laugh about!'"

"I freed myself, as soon as I could, to seek out this soul of a man again. I encountered him at the greenhouses with the famous blue 'miracle grotto,' which formed a single floor of splendid bougainvillea. I found confirmation of what I had already believed to be certain at first sight. I can tell you, my dear, I experienced an hour there of pure, sensual pleasure."

"I've also heard of the famous grotto."

"I didn't really mean that. It was something different. I had the truly rare fortune to be able to talk to one of the most notorious robber-murderers of our criminal history."

"I understand, it must be an exceedingly sensual joy!"

"Indeed it is, my dear. Unfortunately, it's very rare. I admit I was lucky. That is part of everything, and of my craft in particular. It would be positively dreary if one didn't occasionally get lucky, too."

"But how did you know at once that he was a robber, and then—people you know to be robbers, they don't just walk around?"

The host's eyes were wide at this narrative. He had not known a single word of any of this, and now he, too, was not at all sure he could believe any of it, or whether Dagobert was not pulling his wife's leg. Experience spoke against the latter. Dagobert had never before, in his stories, woven in an untruth or an exaggeration. Now, however, the matter sounded terribly romantic, and if I was all true, it was quite shameful that he himself was present as things proceeded, yet he had not noticed the least thing.

Dagobert followed up on Frau Violet's last question, and continued: "About all this, I can easily enlighten you, most gracious, even if it's a little intricate. You are not unaware of the fact that I spend a large part of my free time at the identification office of our police department. This office is closely connected with our police museum, which has become positively unique and exemplary on the continent. The institutions support each other and work hand in hand. So, I am there almost daily, and work quite a lot, learning and teaching, yes, also teaching! The recently-founded detective school is also in close contact with the museum, where the young new blood is trained in police scouting. I now also hold different courses and give the younger aspirants the results of my studies and experiences. Dr. Weinlich, who has made an excellent contribution in particular to the establishment of the Anthropometric Division, and is the head of the whole Search service, is very grateful for my co-operation. For this purpose, the state grants only very inadequate means, and therefore a teacher, who in the course of time has gained some trust, and who is also unsalaried, and only collaborates out of love for the cause, is doubly welcome to him."

"I rather think that not many—"

"That not many such fools can be found, you mean to say, Frau Violet. Please feel free to say it. I am already used to it, and quite amused. What do you want? Everyone has their sport! Just in the last cycle of my lectures, which I held there at the school, the man whom I had discovered at Weisbach's was playing a special role. Trautwein, as he called himself here—probably he had stolen the papers and documents appropriate to this name somewhere, for he was actually Anton Riederbauer—is one of the most dangerous criminals to be kept an account of in the identification department. With his splendid, smooth-headed Caesar's haircut, he is in the most flourishing prime of life, and yet he has already spent the trifle of twenty-three years in jail."

"My goodness!" Frau Violet had turned quite pale at this communication, and Herr Grumbach was also made serious. Now he began to gain confidence in Dagobert again.

"Yes," continued Dagobert, "he's a poster child for our prison system. Judging by his appearance, our jails must be veritable health resorts. The story with him is like this: Twenty-five years ago, he committed a robbery murder—a double murder to be precise. It was a bestial crime, with no mitigating circumstances coming into question. He murdered an old couple, in their sleep, and with brutal cruelty, custodians and caretakers, who had kindly afforded him shelter, to get a hold of their meager belongings. He could not be hanged. He was still too young for the claims of the law. He had reached only eighteen years. The death penalty was not possible, and so he came away with eighteen years' worth of hard time. The eighteen years he served honestly. But this is also the only honest thing that he has done in his life. Then he went free, but was soon recaptured and this time—before one didn't know this—anthropometrically recorded. He had committed a burglary and got five years. He served that time, too, but now Dr. Weinlich is searching for him again, indeed for almost a year now. There is a still a break-in the police haven't solved—that is always very annoying!— and Dr. Weinlich swears that Riederbauer committed it. And he doesn't swear without reason. For he found a fingerprint on the crime scene."

"My God, and poor Weisbach had to end up with such a man!"

"It's truly an irony of fate. In the school, I chose with special care the image of Riederbauer as an object of demonstration for a lecture. In the first place, he was still 'wanted,' so it could be useful if his features were impressed on everyone's mind. And secondly, the head is at all events a gratifying and very interesting demonstration object in several respects. I therefore

93

enlarged these little photographs of him, found in the archive, to life-size in the identification department studio, and these enlargements now hang in the classroom as wallboards for study purposes, on the right-hand wall, the second row from bottom left at the corner."

"Tell me, Dagobert," interrupted Frau Violet, "why did his head seem so interesting and instructive to you?"

"As I told you, my dear, in several respects. I would also have to give you a whole lecture to say it all. In short, therefore, only the following: it is self-evident that we are no less zealous in Lombroso's theory of the born criminal than in the more scientific, practical-oriented works of Prof. H. Gross, among others. The Lombrosian conclusions are combated in our time in many cases and even treated a little condescendingly. But not rightly, as I would like to claim, according to my relevant observations and experiences. The symptoms of degeneracy occur so frequently in the world of criminals that they justify certain conclusions. In this respect, Riederbauer is a splendid exception, which is precisely why it still doesn't prove anything against the rule. As such, however, it is particularly noteworthy. His body is quite regular and well-formed, and his head presents the impeccable type of a caesarean head. At most, which is not at all proven, we should regard this type itself as a suspicious feature.

"Riederbauer's pictures also offer interesting study objects in another respect. He is photographed in profile and full face, with a beard and without beard. Establishing identity solely on the basis of photographs is not so simple a matter as it may seem at first sight. At school, we made very instructive comparisons of heads, which, with unbelievable dissimilarity, proved to be the same, and, on the other hand, images which, although strikingly similar, were not identical.

"Riederbauer's portraits, as those of a 'double murder-robbery,' and of those of a wanted burglar, were, of course, treated with particularly loving care, and even with a certain respect, and now you will understand, my dearest, that it had to be in fact a quiet and heartfelt joy for me to meet this interesting personality so unexpectedly."

"In fact, the most delightful pleasure that can be imagined, to suddenly face a wanted robber-murderer!"

"So now I had him, and now it was a question of how to secure him. While I was talking to the gardener, about botanical subjects, of course, I thought one way and another about how to arrest him. I could not quite make up my mind. For the time being, I only knew what I must *not* do. I must not alarm the house. The whole festivity would have been disturbed, and what carried even more weight, Weisbach is a full-blooded, very nervous and uncommonly anxious gentleman. The sudden fright and the excitement of the great danger in which he found himself could have had a detrimental effect on his health. Just remember: the legendary horseman who crossed frozen Lake Constance died of fright, not cold. And this was perhaps a less anxious gentleman than Baron Weisbach, otherwise he wouldn't have been alone at such a late hour in such a lonely place and in the cold. Weisbach couldn't be the one to decide. The matter had to be done differently, and I decided to make it elegant."

"Dagobert makes everything elegant!"

"Thank you for the compliment. One does make an effort. I was still grasped in the best entertainment when I was fetched by force for breakfast. They had already begun without me and had finally become impatient. Then Baron Fries and young Nettelbach, as the youngest, the Benjamins of the company, had been dispatched to bring me back dead or alive under pain of death. So I was dragged along, although I would have very much liked to chat a little with my new acquaintance. We had indeed quickly become well acquainted with each other."

"Well acquainted!"

Why not? I knew how to behave toward him and speak to him in his own language. On the way through the garden, Baron Fries whispered to me: "Just imagine, Dagobert, my silver cigarette case has gone, gone from my overcoat. And I was so proud of it, first prize in tennis handicap! In the house of Weisbach nothing is stolen, of course, but I could swear that I still had it on my way here! I know for certain that I had smoked in the carriage. What could I have done with the cigarette case after that?"

This was a splendid opportunity to sit on my high horse, and I used it. "Be glad, dear Baron," I replied, "that I am on the spot. According to your information, however, the case seems to have been stolen, but one doesn't steal unpunished when I am nearby. I assure

96

you that before the sun goes down, you shall have your case back, but under one condition—do not betray a syllable!" He promised that, but I had my plan ready. I always need a little stimulus from outside when I am in doubt about a war plan. Young Fries had given me just this stimulus. Now I knew what I had to do.

At breakfast the usual little teasing started on my great passion. People do have some respect indeed, but this doesn't prevent them from occasionally enjoying themselves in their little teasing pleasantries. This time the jokes came as very convenient, and I picked up the subject in order not to let it go. I told the most hair-raising detective stories and the most amazing miracles performed with the help of fingerprinting. The host was enormously interested in these things, and I was most grateful for that. Because I had in fact directed everything at him.

"What a pity that Dr. Weinlich is not here,' I cried regretfully. "He could tell you quite different stories. The man has experience and is one of our most capable criminologists of all."

"A shame that it didn't occur to me," replied our host equally regretfully. "I really should have invited him."

As I was well aware, Dr. Weinlich also belonged to Weisbach's close circle of friends. I used the mood, and continued: "It's twice the pity that he is not here. He would now have a wonderful opportunity to show off his art and prepare a brilliant entertainment for us."

"How so?" everybody was curious to learn, the host

most curious of all.

"Very simple," I explained. "I have stolen something from one of the gentlemen present, purely out of love for the cause, and only to test my skill."

Everyone grabbed their pockets involuntarily and then broke out in unanimous laughter, to apologize to me, in a manner of speaking.

"How wonderful it would be now," I continued, "if he were here, and we could give him the task of finding the wrongdoer."

"That could still be arranged perhaps," cried the host with pleasure. "I'll send him the carriage, and since it's also indeed a business matter, he'll probably get away. I'll write him a few lines, and inform him that it's also official. He could do two good works here at once, first of all to lunch with us, and then arrest a villain. Yes, dear Dagobert, if he succeeds in convicting you, then let us arrest you! We'll not have it any other way. This will be great fun."

Then I had him where I wanted him. The attendant servant brought writing paper—with the crown embossed on it! —and the writing utensils to the breakfast table at our host's behest, and Weisbach was about to begin writing. But then I put myself in the middle: "Gentlemen, we must not ask for anything impossible! Just imagine the situation. I have confessed to you that I have stolen something. But you must not tell him this, otherwise there is no joke at all. That's as it must be, and we cannot, for our part, allow him to suspect one after the other in this illustrious society.

For, I beg your pardon, you all are no less unlikely as thieves than I am. We must therefore offer him some clue. I would suggest that we send him a thumbprint from me. Then we'll soon see what dactyloscopy is all about."

"That is a glorious idea," exclaimed the newly-born baron. "We'll send him the print, will not reveal anything else, and just say, 'Well, now look for the villain!'"

"I don't think that's a very good idea," Grumbach objected. "The print could only be of use to him if he were able to find the corresponding one in his archive. But this is not possible because the archive contains only the fingerprints of notorious criminals. Our friend Dagobert doesn't yet understand this. For what purpose, then, should his print be sent?

The objection of your husband, Frau Violet, was, in general, perfectly justified, since he had just as easily fallen into the trap as all the other members of the revered society. But I was also able to dispel his doubts too."

"How did you go about that?" asked Frau Violet. "To me, too, his objection seems to be perfectly valid."

"Which I have freely admitted. My explanation was the following: Of course, the archive is only for fingerprints of criminals there. Now, however, Dr. Weinlich and I spent several months busy with certain investigations, which so far, unfortunately, have remained completely unfruitful. We wanted, specifically, to investigate whether certain conclusions could be drawn from the image of the criminals' finger lines, so that in the end, perhaps, from the very fingerprints themselves, the criminal disposition might be recognized. To do so, we had to compare hundreds of impressions of notorious criminals with those who were notoriously not criminals. As regards the latter, Dr. Weinlich and myself allowed ourselves to include ourselves, and thus our fingerprints came to be in the archive."

"This is certainly a good explanation, Dagobert," said Frau Violet.

"At least it fulfilled its purpose. But I can tell you, Madame, that this clearing-up was only a great sham. We have, of course, never made such nonsensical studies, and our prints are not, of course, in the archive."

"Now, Dagobert, I really do not understand you!"

"I followed my plan. I wanted a sheet of paper with a fingerprint to be sent to Dr. Weinlich in the letter. I had the paper in my notebook and took it out. The whole company looked at "my" thumbprint with great interest."

"Was it not your print, then?"

"Of course not."

"Then it was...?"

"Of course, Anton Riederbauer, alias Trautwein."

"Yes, did you really need the print?"

"When it comes to the freedom and the whole existence of a human being, my dearest, I do not wish to rely exclusively on my eye, which might have been deceived by a deceptive similarity. Thus, more rigorous evidence had to be brought to the matter."

"How did you happen to have his thumb print?"

"It was not accidental. I had taken him from him before I went to breakfast."

"But you didn't say anything at all about it!"

"I can make good on that."

"That will also be necessary. One doesn't go to a robber-murderer and tell him in all comfort: Be so good as to give me a fingerprint!"

"Very true. Especially not to a person who has already been treated legally in the Identification Office, and who knows the whole rigmarole. So, I had to take refuge in outsmarting him, which, by the way, was not so difficult."

"How did you go about that, Dagobert?"

From the outset I had intended to get the print, and so entangled him in a conversation which took his full attention. We were in the hot-house with the exotic plants, for which I showed a special interest, and about which I requested detailed instructions given to me. On each of the plants hung a little plaque with the exact designation which I wanted to write down. In fact, I gave the pretext of wanting to build a hothouse for exotic plants in my garden. I began to jot things down and soon found this uncomfortable, since there was much to write. So, I put my notepad into his hand and asked him to follow me and always hand me a blank sheet as needed. As a base for writing, I used a notebook, in which I could also supply the pages immediately. Riederbauer, as I noticed with pleasure, had quite dirty hands from gardening. I was very quick to write, and he had trouble keeping up with administering the sheets. These didn't detach easily from the strongly compressed pad. In my zeal, I impatiently urged him to hasten: "Quick, quick!" And then came what I had counted on. In his eagerness to serve, Riederbauer unconsciously dampened his thumb with his tongue, in order to cope with the thin sheets more easily. It was a kind of reflex movement.

"So sorry," he said. "Now the sheet is quite dirty."

"No matter," I replied, and let the sheet fall carelessly, "Let's just move on to the next!"

Now I no longer put the sheets into the notebook, but I left them on the floor next to me for the time being, from which I finally picked them all up. Of course, also in my absent-mindedness the "spoiled one" too. Soon after, I was fetched to breakfast. Before that, however, I had had the opportunity to convince myself that I had got a very excellent thumb print. If it could be played into the hands of Dr. Weinlich without delay, the matter was settled. And so Weisbach wrote his invitation. While he was writing, I went out to let him set the trap. Outside, I hastily scribbled on a sheet of paper: "Very urgent! Confidential! Weisbach has no idea what is going on. Collate the print, and get the man. Bring two elegant but sturdy people. You will find a silver case on him, which you deliver to the company without mentioning the perpetrator. Do not drive up at the main entrance, but at the back at the park gate. You have to look for the gardener. *Re bene gesta*. Appear at dinner without betraying anything. Very Best Regards! Dagobert." When I came back, I pushed "my" fingerprint into the envelope. It had to be treated with caution, and I had given it a protective paper cover— that was my handwritten letter.

Breakfast went very pleasantly, and no less pleasant was the break between breakfast and lunch. Two card parties formed, several men rode and went for a walk, the rest went into the park. I made sure that those remaining behind kept the gardener on his toes. I sent them by installments to the greenhouses to study the exotic natural wonders. Riederbauer had to be the guide incessantly, which brought him a good deal of tips. For me it was only a question of holding him, so that we had no misgivings about not finding him at the end of the intended visit.

We were already sitting at the table when, greeted with general enthusiasm, Weinlich entered. A glance told me that our affair was smoothly arranged. You can imagine the jubilation, Frau Violet, when he showed the stolen case the minute he appeared.

"I certainly do not need to name the perpetrator," he said, mindful of my instructions.

"No, Doctor," everybody cried, laughing gaily, "that

is quite unnecessary!"

They were deliciously entertained. Mostly at my expense. So, a professional criminologist is just something different than a dabbling lover of Dagobert's type! I gladly let it go over me. The mood became more and more cheerful, and I was mocked more and more. What did it matter? I had achieved my purpose. The criminal had been made harmless and captured safely, and that had been done without disturbing the party, and thereby spoiling the festive mood.

We ate and drank well, and the latter certainly not a little, as far as the battered bottle receptacle made a judgment possible. Dr. Weinlich is a brilliant companion and has a splendid singing voice. He was a precentor, and he led us in a chorus. I can tell you, my dearest, that your spouse, when he has a few glasses of sparkling wine, also becomes a very serviceable singer.

Upon the general departure, we took with us Baron Weisbach, who was in the merriest mood of all, and lent him a few tried and true strong young men, who were to continue a little "spinning" with him at "Venedig in Wien," the new amusement park, and should then take him to the Palace of his count son-in-law for the night. I thought that was necessary, because, in his villa he had been deprived of his faithful guardian for the night, and without him, he would have been too much afraid. Tomorrow will be soon enough for him to hear the true story.

"But now," Dagobert concluded, "as regards my most esteemed friend, Grumbach. He heard someone call out when he left, that Dr. Weinlich had had a servant arrested in the Villa, and at once he concluded that I had become very embarrassed. Tell me yourself, Frau Violet, if he could have given me higher praise!"

The Cheat

Andreas Grumbach had always led a quite retired life. His marriage to the actress Moorlank, contrary to the first assumptions of his dissuading friends, had turned into a completely undisturbed and happy one. The blonde Frau Violet ran the household with flawless care and skill, and Grumbach felt so content at home that he didn't think at all of any distractions, although Frau Violet might not have been averse. She was too wise, however, to press for changes where everything otherwise proceeded to all-round satisfaction.

Grumbach had enough work during the day, and so he preferred to spend his evenings at home, which Frau Violet had furnished perfectly to his taste with all circumspection, tact, and taste. Once a week he visited his club, he owed himself that; and for one evening in the week he had a box at the opera, which he owed to Frau Violet. But otherwise they stayed at home, where it was the most beautiful in his view.

They rarely saw guests around them. Dagobert Trostler, the vaunted man-about-town, who was now only pursuing his hobbies in the quiet enjoyment of his pension, hardly counted. He could come and go as he liked. One was always prepared for the old friend of the household, and he belonged, so to speak, to the house. His great passions were often smiled at, but he was too much a philosopher to let himself be troubled by that.

For Grumbach, he had become practically indispensable, by the power of habit, but also in other ways. He was a faithful and caring friend, on whom one could absolutely rely in all of life situations. But he was also a mediator for the external world. He brought the news of the day into the house, made sure that one was kept up to date in the matter of art, and he was able to tell all kinds of robbery and criminal stories, with which one could entertain oneself quite well.

But this idyll had now come to an end, and the Grumbachs were suddenly hurled into the whirl of the social life of the imperial capital and residence, very much against the inclination of the husband, and less so against that of Frau Violet, who now found that she was playing the part that had always long belonged to her, and rightly so.

This was the situation: Baron Friedrich von Eichstedt, head of the old and reputable company Eichstedt & Rausch, was the founder of the Industrialists Club and its annually re-elected president for a full ten years. As the ten years ended, the jubilee was celebrated with great ovations. There was a memorable banquet, to which the wives of the members were also invited. Frau Violet's gown was worth seeing. The great surprise for the President was the solemn unveiling of his portrait painted by Leopold Horowitz for the meeting room. He had, of course, sat for the artist. Splendid speeches were given, and everything was very fine. Only one thing seemed regrettable. The president didn't want any more presidency. He'd had enough; he was finished. He had served for ten years, and now somebody else must take the reins.

There was nothing to be done, and Andreas Grumbach was unanimously elected president in the next General Assembly. There it was, a fine gift. Declining wouldn't do. At home Frau Violet cajoled, and she had even asked Dagobert to calm her husband's doubts. But even without that—it really wouldn't do to refuse. The election meant a distinction as great as a medal or a knighthood. The first club of the city and the club of the heads of the Empire's industries. To this end, one had to be of good lineage, figuratively speaking, which is to say that his personal and business reputation was above all reproach, that his credit was an unrestricted one, and that his wealth was very well-established. For a business man, such an appointment was like being elevated to the nobility.

Such a thing was not to be refused, especially since the honor also had its burden, which made the takeover appear as a duty of honor in two respects. It was well known and had formally become a tradition, through the administration of the first president, that the club leadership was linked to considerable material sacrifice. In Vienna, the clubs have always had a very difficult job. The countless elegant coffee houses that London, the classic seat of the club, doesn't have, offer virtually unbeatable competition with their amenities and comforts. That is why all clubs only flourish temporarily, and then work under a deficit for as long as possible. Nevertheless, the industrialists wanted to have their club, and, of course, from the outset, any doubt about its survival had to be quelled. But since the industrialists were not able to conjure magic either, one relied on each respective president taking care of the honor of the House, that is, to make sure that no deficit would appear.

The membership fees were quite substantial, two hundred guilders a year. There was also income from the gaming enterprise, which, over the year, amounted to twenty thousand guilders. But there was no lack of spending, either. Ten thousand guilders' rent, ten thousand guilders for the staff, ten thousand guilders for heating, lighting, newspapers and other purchases, ten thousand guilders' loss in the kitchen and cellar. Everything had to be first-class, and, at the same time, cheap, to attract and retain the members. And so it went. The expenses are already mounting up.

Now Andreas Grumbach was loaded with all these worries, and that was still not everything. The new honor also entailed representation duties, from which he had formerly had such wonderful peace. Previously he had sat so comfortably aside, and now the social current was drawing him in. If the minister of the Imperial House and Foreign Affairs gave a bash, or the prime minister gave a soirée, if a memorial was unveiled, or a general was buried, or a school was inaugurated, or an exhibition was opened, the president of the Industrialists' Club was invited and had to be there. His presence at the occasion was then always recorded in the minutes of the board meetings for evermore. Then came the private invitations, which one had to reciprocate. In short, things proceeded quite colorfully, and Frau Violet was very pleased.

Baron Eichstedt actually bore most of the blame for the whole thing. First, because he had established the chairmanship, and second, because he had fallen completely in love with Frau Violet—naturally and with all due respect. This was the lady he had long wished for and long sought. His own wife had died, twelve years ago, and until that time, his whole social life had been based in his house. Since then, he had devoted himself entirely to his club, which replaced his home. But now conscience was stirring in him. Things had to change. When his wife died, she left him a single child, a little daughter, Gretl. She was now a young lady of eighteen, whose future one had to think of, after all. He had to see people around him, and he had to introduce the girl into the world. For this, he needed a female friend of his own, who was amiable enough to do the honors by his side at his house on festive occasions, and to chaperone his daughter outside the home with the necessary grace and dignity. He could have found no more suitable person anywhere than Frau Violet. She was a lady of the world who knew how to dress, how to behave, and how to represent herself. Nor was she ever stiff and dull about it, but always well-disposed and lively. Gretl could indeed learn something from her. That she had been an actress was not detrimental to her socially. If, at first, there had perhaps been concern here and there, the weight of her husband's social prestige had very soon set it aside.

But for all that, Dagobert Trostler always joined in. Grumbach wouldn't have given him up at any price, and Frau Violet was so accustomed to him that she would have missed him very much. Thus, when Grumbach became president, Dagobert not only had to enter the club, he also had to acquiesce to be co-opted into the board, at the suggestion of the president. The friendship was a notorious one, and one acted in accordance with it. It was known to please the president when one invited him with his friend.

As criticism follows every great maneuver, so, too, did the critical discussion of it follow at Grumbach's house, even when one returned home so late. Dagobert always had to agree to "a small black coffee and a cigar." Frau Violet wanted it so. One could not go to sleep straightaway. A small chat, a little gossip, a bit of focusing on people - that soothes the nerves wonderfully.

So, the three of them sat once again at an evening hour, taking stock of the newly-finished soirée at Eichstedt's.

"It was, however, very pretty," remarked Frau Violet, who was the interested party.

"It was flawless," corroborated Dagobert, sipping his coffee. "You were simply admirable, Frau Violet, how you did the honors."

"My God, it is so hard when there are so many people!"

"Yes, it was indeed a little too crowded."

"You have nothing to complain about, Dagobert. You are always on the watch with your observations. The more people, the better for you."

"That's not true, Frau Violet. It's better to observe when the crowd is not so great."

"So, no yield today?"

"Oh, on the contrary, a trifle already! I want to know if she loves him too."

"You have such a strange way, Dagobert, of throwing people off with abrupt questions and claims. Who should love whom? And how should I know?"

"Not as abrupt as it seems, most gracious. I merely love occasionally assuming that everybody knows the person, and to waste no time. I mean in reality that if someone could know it, it must be you."

"Slightly clearer, if you please!"

"I saw a pretty little scene in the hall as we left. An actress could have learned from it."

"You make me curious, Dagobert."

"The servants were helping the gentlemen into their overcoats. A young man, undoubtedly the prettiest in the whole company—he has such beautiful melancholy-dreamy eyes—"

"I know now—Baron André, the young attaché."

"At what embassy is he?"

"None at all. He is a diplomat by profession, and now he is waiting for his government to direct him to Petersburg or Madrid."

"Good. I noticed, therefore, that this young man maneuvered it, not without skill, to ensure that not one of the six lackeys came to help him dress, but the only parlor maid in the hall."

"She was there to help the ladies."

"I understand perfectly. Not bad taste. I would have rather had her help me too. I continued to watch. And now comes the little scene. She was most charming. He pushes something into her hand, the tip. There you should have seen the face of the little chamber kitten. It was too charming: In the first moment, perplexity, icy coldness, even indignation. Then a quick glance and immediately bright sunshine. Quickly the arranging hand went over his cloak again, then a friendly smile and a submissive bow. I liked the girl!"

"If only she liked you, Dagobert! And what happened further with your interesting hall studies?"

Frau Violet said this in a not very gracious tone. Friend Dagobert might have known that with a beautiful woman, perhaps any woman, one is very rarely fortunate when particularly delighted with another feminine being. And indeed, when this other being is a parlor maid! Serious researchers have long been in agreement about the fact that parlor maids, may have their aesthetic advantages, but certain things cannot be discussed with women.

"I mean," continued Dagobert, "that this changing and expressive performance by an artist on the stage would have recorded a special applause. During the journey to you, my dearest, I construed the matter then.

The maid first felt the small coin in her hand. Hence the just indignation. The quick glance taught her that it was not a small coin, but a piece of gold. At that—"

"Allow me, dear Dagobert," Frau Violet interrupted him a little impatiently. "Your tipping philosophy may indeed be really quite interesting, but actually it's not what I wanted to know from you."

"I am quite on the job, my dearest, but one has to let a man talk. Gold pieces as tips are not really common among us. In older operas and tragedies, one throws a bag of zechins to the servants, but that is no longer done. These days, only French dramatists are still truly lavish. They usually let their heroes make a tremendous gesture—a million more or less, they do not care a whit. And, in fact, they gladly leave them huge tips. In our bourgeois social life, this is not style. We give a silver guilder, and I mean—"

"But, Dagobert!"

"Do not become impatient with me, my dearest."

"But how can one not be impatient? You wanted to talk about a romance novel in which I was supposed to play a part, and now you give me a lecture about tips."

"I said I had construed the matter in the carriage. The tip story has brought me to the right track. The young man is not stupid—"

"And nobody said he was."

"—And proceeds very methodically. Baroness Gretl is the most gracious and amiable young lady I know.

Who actually introduced him into the company?"

"Gretl's cousins, Fredl, the cavalryman, and Gustl, the ministerial secretary with whom he is intimately acquainted. Incidentally, you must know him from the club, where he has been registered as a guest as long as he has been in town."

"I had not yet noticed him. So he proceeds methodically. He loves Baroness Gretl, and he is certainly not to blame for that."

"How do you know that, Dagobert?"

"At first, I noticed it by—but you must not be angry—how he paid you court, gracious lady."

"Me?"

"You. Indeed. That was quite rightly calculated. You represent the hostess there, and, as I will readily add, with admirable grace and unparalleled prudence. He didn't underestimate your influence. His chances would be bad if he had you against him. He therefore approached you, and, as I noticed with pleasure, not without success."

"What do you mean by that, Dagobert?"

"What I said. You have taken him to your heart."

"Because he's a charming person."

"I agree. One can think of nothing prettier or more amiable than the way in which you, Madame, knew how to mother the two young people, despite the manifold demands."

"Have I done anything wrong with this?"

"Certainly not. It was a special pleasure for me to see how the genuinely feminine impulse of stirring up marriages also worked in you."

"And what does the tip have to do with all this?"

"Not much more than it gave me some ideas. Otherwise, I would hardly have thought further about the whole thing. Methodically, I said. You were won. Some lout among the lackeys could scarcely have been of any use to him; on the other hand, the maid may, under certain circumstances, become a very useful ally."

Now Frau Violet was satisfied. It had, after all, pleased her, how Dagobert had brought out all that, which she had believed that not a soul had noticed.

A few days later, Dagobert was back in Grumbach's house. They were only three at the table, and then they went to the smoking room, where Frau Violet was sitting comfortably by the fireplace at her favorite spot, while the two gentlemen sat down at the smoking table. They sat silent for a while, and then Dagobert began, with a quite innocent expression, as if he were speaking of the most natural and self-explanatory thing in the world. "By the way, do you know, my dear Grumbach, that there is cheating at your club?"

"For God's sake," cried Grumbach, and started up, as if bitten by a tarantula. He had become quite pale. "That is indeed terrible! And you only tell me now?"

"I have only known it myself since this morning, and I didn't want to spoil your appetite before dinner."

"I will resign!"

"That means you do not wish to worry about anything. Your successor should then see how he will deal with the matter."

"I want nothing to do with such matters."

"So, for all you care, is one to simply keep calmly cheating?"

"But Dagobert, don't you see that my situation is terrible?"

'It's certainly not pleasant, Herr President!'

"There will be a scandal out of this!"

"One takes that for granted."

"And the club will perish! What have we not done for the benefit of our civil respectability? With what reassurance did our old gentlemen not supply us with their sons, and now this—the most terrible thing. I shall go!"

"I think you must stay, precisely to save the club."

"I thank you! Whose name will be given in connection with the dirty business? My own! The Grumbach regime! Under its predecessor such a thing was not possible. Save the club? It's as good as lost. It only takes one word of this to reach the public. And how do you mean to prevent that? And everyone who cares for his reputation will retreat. Rightly so. Police, prosecutor, a scandal such as there never was, and I am enthroned as president in the middle of it!"

"It's an evil business, Grumbach, but that is precisely why we must strive not to lose our heads."

"There's nothing left to do once the ball has started rolling. Should I take it on myself, perhaps, to cover up such stories? It's my duty to make the report, and thus pull the club together."

"Well, honestly, I am not knowledgeable enough myself in this case," Dagobert admitted.

"What do you know, Dagobert?"

"For the time being, I only know that something is being played false, nothing more."

"Do you have any evidence?"

"I've got it in my pocket."

He reached into the pocket of his jacket and brought out a deck of cards which he handed over to Grumbach. Frau Violet, who had already begun to weep silently to herself, because, not without reason, she saw her happily achieved social position under serious threat if Grumbach really abdicated, now joined the two gentlemen, and began to examine with her husband the fateful deck. But both were unable to discover anything suspicious.

"The thing is not badly done, indeed," admitted Dagobert, "but it is nevertheless the simplest form of *maquillage*. There are even better methods. This is only the most convenient, and quite sufficient for an audience that is not suspicious."

"So, show us," urged Frau Violet, "how and where these cards are marked."

"But with pleasure, my dearest. But first I want to prove to you that they are really marked. Would you be so kind as to shuffle the deck? Just a bit more! That's it! Did you shuffle well?"

"Certainly!"

"Good. And now, Grumbach, cut the deck. Once again! You cannot be careful enough. And now I will give you a card. How many cards should I give you, dear?"

"Let's say four."

"Well, there you have four cards. Just hold them very carefully, so I cannot see them. Here are four cards for you too, Grumbach. Do you think I could see what I gave you?"

"Impossible!"

"Of course, quite impossible, but you, my dearest, have the Queen of Hearts, the King of Diamonds, Eight of Hearts and Queen of Clubs, and you, Grumbach: King of Clubs, Jack of Hearts, Ace of Clubs and Ace of Diamonds. Is it true?"

It was true.

"And do you now believe," continued Dagobert, "that this knowledge gives me a considerable advantage over my fellow-players?"

"Do I believe it!" cried Frau Violet. "Listen,

Dagobert, you are uncanny to me. You are indeed officially a perfect cheat yourself!"

"I could be, my dear. For everything that pertains to this, I know and master perfectly. By God, one does one's research. There is in fact also literature for this. The excellent French policeman Mr. Cavaillé wrote a very instructive book on cheating. The book by the conjurer Houdini is also entertaining on the same subject. But the most profound book about it, of course, was written by a German who, under the pseudonym of Signor Domino, only concealed himself meagerly. Even a separate magazine was devoted to this noble discipline. It appeared just before the outbreak of the French Revolution, and had the title *Diogène à Paris*. False play also penetrates into wider circles and higher up than is generally assumed. It is asserted with all certainty that Cardinal Mazarin was a cheat. Perhaps that is myth, but it is true and substantiated that in 1885, Count Callado, the emissary of the emperor of Brazil, was indicted in Rome in the course of cheating."

"Listen, Dagobert, but you know everything!"

"Perhaps not only in my opinion, a detective is lost——and what a miserable part he would have to play—if he didn't know and could not tell everything."

"In any case I wouldn't wish to play with you," said Frau Violet, laughing.

"Thank you for your trust, but I wouldn't recommend it. I am in fact a strong player and a polymath. I have playing talent. I don't do much with it, but it's there. I would, therefore, be a very dangerous opponent for anyone, let alone for your naive mind, my gracious one, even without cheating. Because this is so, and because I know everything, I never play, on principal. I am merely a very respected nosy parker, who doesn't make any mistakes in watching, and am considered the supreme and unappealable authority for all matters in dispute."

Grumbach was much too excited and anxious to be able to relish the chatter of Dagobert. He wanted to know how Dagobert had come to the fact that marked cards were being played at the club.

"That was very simple," replied Dagobert. "As a committee member, I have the duty to look after the administration. As far as the kitchen and the cellar are concerned, I have already made tremendous effort. It's all in the finest order, and—I'm sorry to say—the deficit from these operations will remain undiminished for us. Then I also wished to take an interest in the gaming department. This will not surprise you, coming from an amateur detective. There too, as far as accounting is concerned, everything is in order."

"Thank you for such order!" exclaimed Grumbach, bitterly.

"Then an idea came to me," continued Dagobert, "which might not have come to another. I once wanted to check the overplayed cards. So, I had all the card decks, which had been used during the past week, brought to me in the boardroom, locked the door, and then proceeded to checking."

"How many decks were brought to you then?"

Asked Frau Violet.

"Four hundred and fifteen, my dear."

"Lord, you have had a terrible job!"

"It was not so bad. You must not believe that I looked at every single card under the magnifying glass, or else I'd still be there. I took only one card from each deck, admittedly not at random. If the important cards were not marked, then the rest were certainly not either. But if a deck was marked, it would have to be first and foremost those cards on which one mainly depends in the party. Thus, I was able to be finished in three hours."

"And what did you find?" Asked Grumbach.

"As I have already remarked, that there is cheating at the club. I removed six marked decks and put them under lock and key. One of them is this one here."

"You still haven't shown us how they are marked."

"Not so, I think I said it already: *maquillage*, simple make-up!"

"We are not of the discipline, dear Dagobert. You need to talk a bit more plainly with us."

"Well then, listen to me, dear lady. You will be disappointed in how simple the cheat is. Look at the back of this card. It's imprinted and displays a simple pattern, intentionally chosen so as not to give any particular clues to the eye. We have here countless points and small, not completely closed circles. The cheat now chose the following method: he took a fine sewing needle, dipped its tip into pure, colorless wax, made liquid by heating. Then, at a certain point, he gently pricked the back, but not so much so that the tip would penetrate through the card. As lightly as he stabbed, the tip has still caused a small depression, and an atom of wax was fixed in it."

"But it's impossible to feel it with the fingertips," remarked Frau Violet, immediately trying to make the test.

"If he had wanted to rely on his sense of touch, he would have tried another method. There are such, but they are more dangerous and therefore less advisable."

"But he cannot see this tiny dot," continued Frau Violet, again trying to get to the bottom of the secret.

"You can see them very well. Just let the light play on the back!"

"Yes, indeed," cried Frau Violet, delighted. "Here you can see it quite clearly—a matte dot!"

"That's the whole trick. The card paper has a sheen, and in the light reflection, a dull dot makes itself easily noticeable, however only for those in the know. Everything else is self-evident. You see, here there are eight small circle lines in a row, and there are twelve rows. A deck could thus be made up of ninety-six cards, and the artist would still not be in a quandary over where he should put his dot for each card once he has established his system. Not much is demanded of his memory. The first row goes for Hearts, the second for Diamonds and so on. He starts with the king, then the queen -the whole thing is so cheeky it's almost childish."

Grumbach was by no means as interested in the details as his wife. He was plagued by the critical situation in which he and the whole club had plunged. His thoughts moved in a very different direction.

"I am only happy, Dagobert," he began, "that I now have you at hand. You are the man to put an end to the cheating. "

"I flatter myself, indeed, that the right man is in the right place at the right time. I pledge to give you the crook in a few days!"

"You are too kind, Dagobert, and I thank you most sincerely."

"I thought so."

"If I know him, I must deliver him to the court. I must, it cannot be otherwise. And then we'll have a public scandal with all its consequences."

"I think so, too. But what else would you have me do?"

"Get rid of the rogue in silence. He should look for his rope elsewhere. No man must ever learn even a peep of the matter, and as far as I am concerned, I never wish to hear of it again."

"*Bon*! It shall be provided."

Four days later the three of them sat together again in Grumbach's house. At the table, where the servants were going to and fro, only indifferent things were spoken of: the soirées at Eichstedt's, the next ladies' evening to be held at the club, and so on. But when they were sitting in the smoking-room, safe from disturbances by the staff, and Dagobert was preparing to continue chatting harmlessly about the everyday events, Grumbach could no longer hold his tongue, and burst out with the question that was uppermost on his mind: "Well, Dagobert, how does it stand?"

"With what?"

"Don't be like that. You know."

"You do not mean the—the certain affair?"

"Of course I mean that! What else could I mean?"

"I thought that one was not to discuss that with you at all!"

"Do not be childish, Dagobert, I must know what's going on!"

"I have fulfilled your commission, of course. The matter is settled. You can relax: it's all made right."

"Thank God!" cried Grumbach with a sigh of relief. "So, I can really sleep peacefully again?"

"Like a marmot. No one will ever know about it. It would have to be the gentleman himself that speaks, for which I naturally cannot vouch, but I believe it's not very likely."

"You must tell us," now urged Frau Violet.

"But your gentleman husband doesn't allow it!"

"Nonsense, Dagobert. Tell us!"

"There is not much to tell, at least nothing dramatic, since I naturally had to follow your orders. I had to make sure that cheating no longer happens. That has been achieved."

"I am terribly curious how you did that," interrupted Frau Violet.

"The matter was not difficult from the start, and it went even more easily than I had imagined. First of all, my dear, I had to work out for myself how the fraud was done. The cards had obviously been prepared beforehand, but how were they smuggled onto the card table? The easiest way to do this would be if one of the servants handling the cards were in on the cheat. With us, the setting is such that a silver cup with three packs of cards is placed on a low stool, at each table. The gentlemen like to take a fresh pack once they have played an hour with a deck. The servant would therefore have to go to the relevant table and to the company in question—"

"Which group was it?" Asked Grumbach.

"No idea! Among the three decks, only the marked pack had to be served. This would have made the matter quite unobtrusive."

"And was it done like this?" questioned Frau Violet.

"No, my dear. Our artist works without assistants. It's safer and cheaper. An accessory is always a danger, and neither does one wish to have too many expenses in the business."

"I do not understand at all," remarked Grumbach, "how one of us could hit upon this idea, when I, fundamentally and with all due rigor, forbid gambling in the club. I will not tolerate it!"

"A very beautiful principle, without a doubt, and you are very right, my dear Grumbach. But, in practice, there is a snag. The ban must exist, of course. Indeed the state decrees it, too, although such paternalism is less pleasing to me there. If a couple of idlers are stupid enough to engage in such sport, I do not know whether one has the right or the duty to catch them by the tail. If one doesn't leave them to it, they will certainly be able to find some other, no less extensive stupidity."

"One must protect the people from themselves," remarked the president.

"Maybe the economically weak. There is no protection for those weak in spirit and character."

"No philosophy now, dear Dagobert," Frau Violet pleaded. "Rather, tell us more. I was never so curious!"

"Immediately, my dear, just one remark. The instinct to gamble, once it exists, is perhaps grounded in human nature, and when it's actuated, it can easily become more and more dangerous if it happens, of necessity, secretly, rather than in the open and under the control of society. But this is only by the way. The ban must, of course, stay in force for the sake of decency. In our case, gambling was not necessary at all. One played with chips. How highly the gentlemen value them is entirely their own business, and no one else needs to know. Our artist could also earn his three or five hundred guilders a day playing the most innocent and most permissible game, without any stir. That is, I think, rather something!"

"One ought to execute such a person!" Frau Violet interjected.

"I zeroed in on the club servants. You will be pleased to hear, Grumbach, that they have absolutely nothing to do with this matter. I studied them especially closely without their noticing. They are completely uninvolved."

"Pleased to hear it," Grumbach confirmed.

"Now I had to consider further. I'd dissected six decks, three Tarot and three French decks, all marked according to the same system. I had inspected one week's material. Now I came to the following conclusions: First, there is only one cheat. Second, the cheat has used only one marked deck every day. This is also explainable. For, thirdly, he had to put the prepared deck himself on the stool and spirit away a different deck in his pocket. Not an easy problem, I admit, but at least it is solvable. The young gentlemen usually appear in tailcoats. For usually, they either have a dinner behind them, or some other social obligation. With the help of a top hat and a silk handkerchief, which can be placed unobtrusively on the card cup and from there removed equally inconspicuously, the problem can be solved. With three players, the counterfeiter always had two chances to sit next to the stool. With some assiduity, he had all the chances for himself. No attention is paid to the choice of seats. It doesn't matter. He could even be courteous to one of the partners, and then only needed to preempt the other."

"You were convinced from the outset," asked Grumbach, "that it must be a young man?"

"Yes. One of our old, well-to-do businessmen wouldn't engage in such things. There would be too much at stake. No, it must be a devil-may-care rascal, some lost son."

"Now, finally, come out with your revelation, Dagobert!" the housewife exhorted impatiently.

"Imminently, my dear," replied Dagobert quietly, looking at the clock. "I deliberately hesitated a little, because I now expect a disturbance, a small incident. Seven o'clock on the dot! I should be surprised, I must say, and very unhappy with unpunctuality in this case."

"So what do you expect?" Frau Violet asked curiously.

"A little sign of life of the cheat."

"I hope you do not mean that he will be kind enough to honor us with his visit?"

"I didn't ask for that."

"What else?"

"I ordered him to send a penance of five thousand crowns to the president at seven o'clock in the evening. Ah, he seems to have been really punctual. What's up,

Peter?"

The last words were for the servant who had just entered. There was a porter outside with a letter, which he had to hand over to Mr. Grumbach personally. The man was let in. Grumbach slit the large and sturdy envelope which had been given to him. It contained five one-thousand crown notes and no other written communication, nor was an address on the envelope.

"Who sends you?" Grumbach demanded.

"Forgive us, dear friend," chimed in Dagobert, then turned to the messenger. "Are you paid?"

"Yes indeed, Your Grace."

"Then you can go. Just say: 'It's done.' Nothing else. Adieu!"

When the porter was gone, he continued: "You must excuse me, Grumbach, that I intervened there, but it could not be otherwise. For I am also involved, in fact, and if that's the case, I must at least adhere to fair play. I have imposed some obligations on the man. He has fulfilled them, in part. He will yet fulfill them. With this I have accepted tacitly, as a return service, not to betray him."

"One doesn't make pacts with criminals!"

"That's right. But then I should have handed him over to the police. You didn't want that. So, a way out had to be found. In any case, it's not a question of punishing a man, even a criminal, twice for a thing: first to pillage him in private, and then hand him over to the court. That wouldn't be fair."

"But who is the unhappy man?" Asked Grumbach excitedly.

"How am I to know?" replied Dagobert with a very innocent expression.

"That beats everything. Who else would know?" cried Grumbach.

"I give you my word of honor, Grumbach, that I do not know."

Frau Violet looked at Dagobert open-mouthed.

"You do not know, you give your word of honor. And one should believe that? And here are the five thousand crowns! Dagobert Trostler, are you out of your senses?"

"Oh, the five thousand crowns—they're only a surprise for you, my dearest. You see, I always think of you. Apart from that, I'm really not a warlock. It's all very natural. Grumbach didn't want to know the villain. I also preferred not to have to make his personal acquaintance and to avoid a personal encounter. I should have felt obliged to box his ears, at least. That would have been the least thing to come from me. And, you understand, you do not like to be upset for no reason. So, I preferred to keep to our plan to not expose the man, to avoid the scandal, and only to put a stop to his further fraud."

"And how did you do that?"

"It was not a special feat. I knew that the crook had to bring the prepared decks himself, indeed two decks, as he had to be prepared for both French and Tarot decks. He could only bring only one deck into use, and he could not know in advance which one. It didn't seem likely that he would carry two decks on his person. In a tight, elegant salon suit, that would have been easy to notice. So, when everyone was at work playing, I set off for the cloakroom, and, as if I were looking for my overcoat, I ran both hands down on all the coats hanging there. I snapped so terribly roughly at a servant who asked me helpfully whether I was looking for something, that he immediately evaporated without a trace. Then I found what I was looking for."

"A deck of cards?"

"I felt it was a card deck from the outside. I reached into the pocket. The cards were hidden under a silk handkerchief, so they could not be seen from the outside. I took the cards. A short examination in the boardroom convinced me that I had got the right man—or the right coat. Now the big question was: what to do? In view of the circumstances, I decided to take the following route: I hastily wrote a letter, which I now put into the pocket in lieu of the cards."

"What did you write in the letter, Dagobert?" Frau Violet asked agog.

"I can quote it literally: 'I have the evidence in my hand. Two conditions: 1. You will not enter the club any more. 2. The president will receive five thousand crowns as a charitable donation to the Association for Released Convicts next Tuesday at seven o'clock in the evening, on the dot.""

"The Association for Released Convicts," cried Frau Violet, delighted.

"I had to impose a penance on him, and I decided on the sum mentioned at a guess, although of course I cannot know how much he has taken from his victims. I gave him the time of three days, because I assumed that it was quite possible that a player mightn't have any money at the moment, but that he might get it in three days, if necessary. You can rely on that from gamblers."

"Dagobert, you think of everything!"

"I'm not finished yet, most gracious. We wanted to avoid further developments. So, I was not allowed to search for the victims, to replace their losses either in whole or in part. In doing so, the whole story would have had to come out. I decided, therefore, to consider the Association for Released Convicts. For two reasons: first, to make you happy, since you are one of the most zealous board members of the association, and second, because I thought it simply right and proper. Indeed, I thought to myself, if the man is already handing over the money, he should at least have the opportunity to benefit from it, if only indirectly. "

"Dagobert, you are a humorist!"

"By confronting him with the conditions, I have made a contract with him, and I am implicitly obliged not to betray him. So you see, Grumbach, it wouldn't have been loyal to quiz the servant about the sender. By the way, you may rely on it that it would serve no use. He was so clever that he didn't dispatch the messenger himself, but used the service of an intermediary, whose personal description would be of no use to us."

Grumbach would have liked to know who the deceiver was who had desecrated the club, but he knew that Dagobert had a hard head, and wouldn't be driven further than he wanted to go. Besides, he was very pleased with this solution, because it prevented the public scandal that would otherwise have been unavoidable.

Dagobert didn't appear for a few days, and only came back to pick up Frau Violet for a soirée at Eichstedt's. Grumbach, on business, only followed an hour later. During the trip, Frau Violet came back to the subject of the cheat. She was very interested in the case.

"Dagobert," she began, "I do not believe you haven't found out who it is. This cannot have left you any peace."

"I have found it out, my dearest, but do not betray me to your husband."

"That is dear of you, Dagobert, that you will tell me."

"I didn't say that, and neither will I do so."

"Well, then, what am I not to reveal?"

"That I know it. Otherwise he will torment me, and it would be useless."

"Why do you not wish to tell me now?"

"There are serious reasons for you not to learn."

"I do not understand that, Dagobert."

"It's not necessary, my dear."

"But, since you have found it out, you can tell me."

"Oh, well, so that you don't have any exaggerated ideas about my detective art. This didn't require any special cunning. I knew that the servants in the cloakroom always allot the same number to members and permanent guests. That is very handy indeed. I had only to inquire, therefore, to whom the relevant number belonged, to which the topcoat was attached."

"That simple?" Said Frau Violet, a little disappointed. She had imagined it much more romantic. "Tell me one more thing, Dagobert. Did you not fear that you might drive the man to suicide when you sent him that letter?"

Dagobert shrugged.

"I wouldn't have thought it a misfortune, and I wouldn't have felt my conscience weighted."

"You're terrible, Dagobert. But he also could have retaliated on you."

"I had anonymously written what I otherwise wouldn't have written at all. If I had named myself, I could not have been silent about the matter."

"One more thing, Dagobert. Didn't you suppose he was going to flee from your letter, before he paid the high sum as repentance?"

"I guessed right away that he wouldn't flee, and now I know for sure. He still has a major deal planned, which he will only abandon in the worst case. But here, we've arrived. Allow me to get out first."

They had arrived as the first, but soon guests were pouring in, and Frau Violet did the honors in her charming way. Dagobert sought out Baroness Gretl.

"Baroness Gretl!" he began. "Will you give me two minutes?"

"With a thousand joys, many more, Herr Dagobert!" She called him Dagobert, like most people. Many didn't even know that it was not his surname.

"But undisturbed," he continued.

"Then let us sit down in those window alcoves."

"That is not undisturbed enough for me."

"Then come to Papa's study. There we can negotiate the greatest secrets."

They sat down in the study, and Dagobert ran his hand over his St. Peter's forelock, as he began again: "Baroness Gretl, I must grieve you."

"Nothing bad comes from you, Herr Dagobert."

"God willing, you won't take it hard! Baroness Gretl, you are interested in a young man."

"Oh God, Herr Dagobert, now you come to me with this! You will now prove to me that he is penniless. I know it all already, I know it from his own lips. He does not conceal it, and I, perhaps, do not care either way!"

"No, Baroness, I didn't want to discuss that. I am not a philistine, and I would only be pleased with your bravery. You do not need to be determined by shameful money considerations."

"I wouldn't do it even if I had to, Herr Dagobert."

"Dutifully put, Baroness Gretl! If the young man were only decent and hard-working, and incidentally a handsome man—"

"Is he not!" asked Baroness Gretl, laughing.

"Oh, he has wonderful eyes! But there can be no question that he would be unworthy of you."

"What are you trying to say?"

"That he is perhaps all those things, except not a decent man."

"Herr Dagobert, one must be able to prove such a thing!"

"Of course one must."

"Then prove it!"

"No, Baroness, I will not. It would be an ugly memory for you all your life. Nor should your father know. He would always feel it as a stain on his honor—"

"Herr Dagobert!"

"—As a disgrace that such a man has come and gone in his house."

"And I am supposed to believe your word?"

"Not quite, Baroness. We shall be silent about the qualities of the young man in our mutual interest. I hope to convince you in this way."

"And if not?"

"Then I will save you against your will. I have already once pulled a suicide out of the water, who then assaulted me. It happens. I simply do not tolerate the man to extend his hand to you again, to direct another word at you. I will not tolerate it. I wish to tell you what will happen in the next quarter of an hour that may serve you as full proof. At the moment when one sits down at the table, a servant will hand over this letter to that gentleman. Read it, Baroness."

Baroness Gretl read:

"I order you to leave the company immediately and without greeting. I further command you to leave Vienna within the next twenty-four hours, and never again to be seen in this city, otherwise, the police! Dagobert Trostler. Vienna 1, Tuchlauben 2.1."

"This is horrible!" said Baroness Gretl tonelessly, when she had read. She had gone quite pale, and she looked, bewildered and helplessly, at Dagobert.

"Do you think, Baroness," resumed the latter, "that a decent man can accept this? If he still has a spark of honor in his body, or the least remnant of a good conscience, then he must slap me instantly—you see, I have signed my name fully—or he will immediately send me his witnesses, and I must duel for life with him. None of this will be the case. He will slink away like a beaten dog."

Baroness Gretl sat pale and mute, but she bravely pushed back the streaming tears. But then, something like determination glowed in her eyes.

"Good," she said. "If he acquiesces, he is a lost man!"

"He's lost, Baroness, and he doesn't deserve pity. It hurts me that I had to hurt you. Do you believe I acted as I had to act as your friend and as the friend of your house?"

"Yes, Herr Dagobert, I believe that."

The events took place exactly as Dagobert had previously announced. Calligraphic cards on the covers indicated each person's place at the table. Dagobert had previously placed his card between the places of Baroness Gretl and Baron André. When one went to the table, a servant handed Baron André a letter, which he put in his pocket unread. The servant allowed himself, according to the received orders, to remark that the letter was very urgent and that prompt notice was expected. The Baron opened the letter and quickly read through it. Then he bowed, as if to speak to Baroness Gretl. Dagobert whispered softly but very firmly: *"Allons donc—sans adieu!"*

The Baron straightened up and left the room silently. The company scarcely noticed his exit, and the party went on undisturbed.

The Mysterious Box

After a gentle afternoon nap, Dagobert was busy choosing a fresh necktie, which promised a considerable effect, when the servant handed him a card on a silver plate. With a quick glance he read on it a name that was completely unknown to him.

"I am to tell my lord," the servant hurried to explain, "that the gentleman has been sent by His Excellency, Count Anzbach."

From Count Anzbach! Dagobert widened his eyes. He was accustomed to consorting in the best social circles and was not easily impressed with a name or title, but His Excellency Count Anzbach—that was something special, a class of its own. This was, so to speak, the first nobleman of the empire. It was known of him that he—perhaps the only one in the whole empire—had to rejoice in the wholehearted trusted personal friendship of a very high gentleman. It was even asserted that, without it ever having been possible to ascertain with complete certainty, that the two men were in the habit of addressing one another informally when in private dealings, with no witness present, like other mortals when friendship binds them.

The count was very important, and carried great

weight, and what he did, he did always in grand style, in short, a singular phenomenon. First, a great philanthropist and, indeed, an exception to this in the Austrian High Court, which in general does not feel the need to prove itself in the field of humanitarianism by means of special works. It was known that Count Anzbach kept his own office with three secretaries, who had only to deal with the charitable obligations that pressed on him. Each of the day's posts brought him stacks of requests, prospectuses and projects. All this had to be examined, and, as the technical expression goes, "researched" before a report was made to him and his decision was known.

An almost immeasurable fortune enabled him to intervene any time where real distress called for real help, and no unhappy man was rejected, as long as he was proved worthy of support. It was said that the count's annual budget for charity was to be expressed by seven digits. But he could also practice good deeds with improvements, work and jobs, and not only with money. As one of the greatest industrialists and landowners, and a respected head of a leading party among the high-ranking, he was a wealthy man who could better care for worthy people than anyone else.

All this shot through Dagobert's head when the servant gave him the surprising report, and aroused his curiosity to learn what precisely this man wanted of him. So, he quickly finished dressing, which caused him a bit of trouble in subduing his unruly St. Peter's haircut, and getting his already somewhat grayed beard to the accustomed flawless façade.

A young man came in.

"His Excellency is requesting the honor of Herr Dagobert's visit. It is an important matter."

An important matter from this side! Dagobert felt flattered in self-love, but even so there was something that annoyed him. He is not the man who is simply fetched. One has to make an effort, if one wants something from him.

It was as if the young man had read the thoughts on his face, as he immediately went on: "Excuse me, Herr Dagobert, if I only now present what I should have begun with, with the apology of His Excellency not to submit his request in person. It had its very particular reason - "

"That really would not have been necessary," said Dagobert, quickly coming around. "Tell me, Mr... Mr..."

He looked at the card which he had put down.

"Erdmann, Gustav Erdmann is my name," the messenger hastened to help.

"Right, Mr. Erdmann. Are you in the service of the Count?"

"I am his private secretary."

"Gosh, a fine career for such a young man! How long have you been in that position?"

The young man acted as if he had ignored the question.

"As far as I know," continued Dagobert, Baron von

142

Goth is the Count's private secretary."

"I am the private secretary."

"Is Baron Goth no longer at the house?"

Again, the young man gave no answer. He seemed determined not to answer any questions at all.

Dagobert made another attempt: "Do you know anything, Mr. Erdmann, about what is the occasion for my visit?"

Again, no answer.

"Young man, I like you," said Dagobert now, smiling, placing his hand on the secretary's shoulder. "A private secretary should not be drawn out. If I tried it, it was not an error of education or tact, but simply founded in my hobby, I may almost say, in my profession. Detectives must be as curious as journalists. I will tell His Excellency that you have done well."

While he was speaking, Dagobert had pressed on the electric switch, and he now gave orders to the servant, who appeared silently, for his carriage to be harnessed immediately.

"I travelled by automobile," said the secretary quickly at this point. "If Herr Dagobert would be so kind as to ride with me..."

"Done!"

Five minutes later, Count Anzbach received Dagobert in his study.

"Your Excellency wished me—here I am!"

"And I sincerely thank you for coming, Herr Dagobert. I would like to request your services, and it would have been better had I first paid you my respects, but—"

"But, Your Excellency, let us stop!"

"No, I must justify myself. It is a matter of quite extraordinary importance to me. I should like to say that it is the most important issue ever in my life."

"All the more acutely do I feel the recognition of Your Excellency's wishing to trust me."

"It was obvious. I have always read your friend's reports of your achievements with interest, and my honorable friend, President Grumbach, has also told me so much about your deeds that I had to put the greatest value on winning your strength. If I had sought you out, I should have had to present my request. We would have started talking, and you yourself will most likely admit that this was not the right thing to do. You should receive the first impressions here at the site of the events. I wanted to avoid anything that could have been confusing."

"Your Excellency proves with this statement that you rightly assess the whole detective profession correctly, and would probably have become an excellent detective, if you had not preferred to remain the 'first nobleman of the empire.'"

"Truly," replied His Excellency, laughing, "I almost believe myself that I had the right disposition for some sort of vocation. I ask you—when one meets so many people who, in one way or another, have one thing in mind, when one finds oneself one's whole life literally in a defensive position against a mass attack, one's perceptions of people and circumstances become sharpened. And this view—I believe that is the most important requirement of the fine art of detection. But now to the point. But first you must take a cigar, so I may also smoke. One speaks better thus."

"Thank you, Your Excellency, mine is already lit. So let's hear it."

"Good, let's begin. So, last night—you must be careful, Herr Dagobert, your cigar is burning badly—so, last night my fire-and-burglar-proof money box was robbed."

"Your Excellency wishes to take me by surprise with an explosive effect."

"I assure you, Herr Dagobert, that nothing is further from my mind than showmanship. I simply report the fact that my money box has been robbed."

"As far as I can see, Your Excellency is not particularly upset by this fact. Perhaps it would not be appropriate if I were to get upset by it."

"Excitement is not at all useful, neither for me nor for you, Herr Dagobert!"

"Very true. But since it is perhaps the most important matter of your life—was it not so? I should think—"

"Indeed, that was true—it is true. So important that I do not know how I could continue living if your skill fails to save me. Yes, Herr Dagobert, you can take that literally: save me!"

"I cannot imagine that a treasury for Your Excellency could be of such key significance. Was the amount so very great?"

"No, Herr Dagobert. That wouldn't upset me. You know that I own a couple of dozen estates, castles, palaces, houses—of course, all of them unaffected. That can't be carried away by a mere burglary."

"It's not, then, the material value that is so important. This, at least in one way, provides a certain calm."

"On the contrary! This is precisely the cause of the great alarm."

"If that is the case, then, from my professional point of view, I have only one, preliminary remark, Excellency. It is now four o'clock on the dot after noon and we sit comfortably over a cigar. The burglary or theft was committed at night. Your Excellency undoubtedly learned of the crime in the morning, yet seem not to have been in a great hurry to start the investigation. I scarcely need to point out that much valuable time has now been wasted, and that all further measures which might lead to success have been made considerably more difficult."

"Your accusation is only partly justified, Herr Dagobert. I did in fact do everything in the early morning, or, to express myself very precisely, at seven

146

o'clock in the morning, that seemed necessary, indeed indispensable, in the given case."

"May one ask?"

"Of course you may! I must speak plainly. I immediately informed the police, and I telephoned the High Commissioner, Doctor Thaddeus Ritter von Skrinsky."

"And he's been here?"

"Has been here, did an on-site inspection, established the facts. He is quite confident and has given me great hope. He is anxious to turn his very special attention to the case, and, I suppose, is already engaged in the investigation full throttle."

"Then—"

"So you may rest easy, Herr Dagobert!"

"No, Your Excellency, it would be futile. You undoubtedly acted rightly when you informed the police immediately, but my co-operation must now be excluded."

"But your cooperation is of the utmost value to me!"

"It can't work, Your Excellency. It would be quite stylistically incongruous to have the case taken on by two different entities at the same time. Nothing orderly can come out of it. They get in each other's way. One can spoil what the other believes to have made good. The quarry is disturbed and frightened and finally slips away, merely because the hunters were standing in each other's way. It really doesn't work!"

"I have let you finish speaking, my dear Herr Dagobert, but now you must do me the favor of listening, too. Our situation is currently an embarrassing one. I have foreseen it, and fully appreciate your legitimate artistic pride. "

"That is not the matter here!"

"It is, it is, dear friend, and rightly so! I simply ask you to be gracious enough to not take me for a fool."

"But Your Excellency!"

"Could you really believe I expected something from Skrinsky? Could you suppose that I myself would not have thought of it as an immense insult to you from the outset, if I turned first to a Mr. Skrinsky, and then asked for your kind co-operation?"

"But that's what's happened, isn't it?"

"Because it had to be! It would have been an insult— under normal circumstances. Here, however, that's not the case. The circumstances gave me the indispensable duty to report to the police. This had to happen for my own cover which is becoming rather necessary. It could be that the omission of official notice, which was legally required, would subsequently be made an unpardonable lapse to the case, and I would then have no case at all. You must understand that, Herr Dagobert!"

"I'm beginning to understand."

"You'll understand me even better in a moment. My

case is not at all suitable for a police investigation, and nothing will ever be forthcoming from one, for the simple reason that I have never given the critical clue to the authorities, or to anyone else but you. Does that reconcile you?"

"I was not offended, Your Excellency."

"You had reason to be. I hope, however, to get you on my side. So, on the one hand, I had the duty of informing the police; on the other, the very urgent wish that it would come to nothing. In this predicament, I could not do anything more sensible than having Skrinsky come to me. For he—I hope you will agree with me with utter conviction—is notoriously and undoubtedly the most inept of all our detectives."

"Oh, yes!"

"I also enjoined him so tightly with duties of prudence and absolute silence that, even if he had Dagobert's genius—"

"Your Excellency is too kind."

"—he could never get results. You see, dear friend, you can rest reassured. He will never cross your path. So, may I count on you?"

"I am at your service, Your Excellency."

"A thousand thanks! Now we can begin the work."

"After everything I have hitherto heard, it would be no use if I wanted to make an on-site inspection. Is the purloined sum significant?"

"Significant is a relative term. Two hundred and forty thousand crowns were taken."

"So, insignificant then."

"You flatter, but I admit that the loss does not worry me."

"I suppose you suspect someone?"

"My private secretary has been missing since this morning."

"Baron Goth? And since this morning, Your Excellency has had another private secretary?"

"That's how it is."

"He seems to be a capable young man. He made the best impression on me."

"I usually have competent people around me, but they are sometimes a little dangerous. I have a tendency to oblige people through gratitude. It often happens to me that derailed or shipwrecked existences, noblemen, officers, and so on, seek rescue with me. This always gives an uncomfortable alternative. Either I help them on their legs, or they put a bullet in their heads. There is usually no third possibility. I therefore help where I think that salvation is really still possible. Now, unfortunately, it is not usually done with money donations. That would be easiest and most convenient, but also the least practical. People must be hooked into a job, into a profession. If not, the uncomfortable alternative is to be employed anew in a short time. I fear, Herr Dagobert, that these remarks will bore you a little."

"I beg you to continue, Your Excellency, I listen attentively."

"But I must present these things to you to make you understand the whole context. Now the difficulty begins. Usually the desperate situation has not been brought about without fault of its own. How, then, am I supposed to recommend men, whom I know to have misdeeds on their conscience, which are often very serious, but not so bad that they should get the death penalty, and that would lead to the inevitable suicide, so how could I recommend *them* to other people? That will not do. So, I have no other choice than to hire and provide for them myself. And so, from time to time, I see myself surrounded by a cadre of employees at whom every reasonable man would apprehensively shake his head."

"Perhaps not wrongly, Your Excellency!"

"I am also prepared to become the victim of a catastrophic experience."

"Such a case seems to have come."

"Baron Goth himself suffered such a failed existence, a degenerate rake. He had not actually done anything dishonorable, he had only squandered. So, I could recommend him, without having anything to hide. I spoke with the Director General of the Central Bank. He had the man come in, examined his abilities, which greatly satisfied him, and thereupon gave him a position of trust. I could observe Baron Goth's activity at close range. I am, in fact, the President of the

Governing Board of the Central Bank. This is actually an honorary position, but I am not accustomed to regard my honorary positions –there are quite a few of them—merely as such. I take a hands-on approach, and especially at the Central Bank, I checked diligently that everything was in good order. It runs large business ventures. There is something of a businessman in me. So, I was quite on the ball. Baron Goth, as presidential secretary, frequently came to my residence, whether to give me confidential communications from the Directorate, or to obtain my instructions or decisions in special cases. This went on for about a year in the most beautiful order, but then unpleasant rumors began to circulate about the baron. Again, nothing really defamatory, but nevertheless quite unpleasant. He was up to something again, and the talk emerged about it. Something had to be going on. I was morally responsible, and he seemed a danger to the bank. There was no plausible excuse to chase him away, and my personal voice would not have answered. After all, he had so far proved to be capable, reliable, and efficient. I made short work of it and asked him to join me as a private secretary, doubling his salary."

"That's just like you, Your Excellency!"

"He could be useful to me, and I could keep a much closer eye on him, and if finally something fatal should happen, it was better it should happen to me than to the bank. My application was accepted, and I gave the bank a shortened notice period of one month. I used the time to get full information about the baron's private life and relations. And now, Herr Dagobert, it is becoming quite difficult for me to keep talking. We see each other today for the first time, and I want to speak to you as I wouldn't speak to any man in the world, not even my most cherished friend. Nor can I even be called upon to be a friend. I hope to be able to do so in the not-too-distant future."

"As for me, Your Excellency, you may certainly call me your friend," said Dagobert.

"I am happy," replied the Count, stretching out his hand to Dagobert, "and so I will speak as a friend to a friend, a man to a man, a gentleman to a gentleman, so unreserved is my confidence that I will not even impose the burden of secrecy on you."

"Very unnecessary, Your Excellency, needless to say."

"Again, I must—you will think I am quite talkative, a man who gets carried away and rambles— must go a little farther, but I must, if you are to see everything clearly. You know that I occasionally surround myself with quite doubtful elements, and I believe you have called this a dangerous experiment."

"I do not know if I said it, but I thought it, at any rate!"

"Well, often such an experiment is unsuccessful, but sometimes it succeeds, and then occasionally one has an experience which would not otherwise have ever happened. Very strange and surprising. In this way, I took on a man, who has become a servant, a slave of all legendary loyalty and devotion. To the extent that, if I had the cravings of the Greats of the Renaissance, I could calmly command him: get me this or that from the world, and in a few hours, it would be done. And if he had been indicted, he would have let his head be cut off without betraying his commissioner with a word. This was a young hussar officer from a good family, who had also gotten into an extremely critical situation. The case was much, much more serious than the one with Baron Goth. If I hadn't interfered, there really was no alternative for him but a bullet in the head. To recommend him to other people was unthinkable. He was completely unskilled. He could have been used as a stable master or trainer at most, but these posts were occupied in my household, and one does not send old, tried and trusted people away to make an uncertain experiment. Where there's a will, there's a way. I finally found him something. I own several cars, and if I have to, I can always make room for a new chauffeur. So, I had him trained, then he took his prescribed examination, and now he has been in my service for six years. We speak very little to each other, but every day I quietly thank chance or fate that I've found such a person. I know he's watching over me and I feel safe. He has no other interest in life than to express his gratitude to me in his silent manner."

"So, an exception!"

"Yes, and a peculiar one. When I thought of taking the Baron into my house, I first I wanted to know more about him. So, I took my chauffeur aside, and instructed him: You, Andor—it was his explicit and comprehensible request to be called only by his first name, and he had insisted that I should address him informally—so, you, Andor, tell me how it stands with Baron Goth and what is really going on with him."

"Do you know, Your Excellency, that I envy you the man? I might need such a person like a bite of bread."

"He brought it all out—more than I liked! The baron had indeed resumed his lavish life, and the motive for this was not exactly an unusual one."

"Probably divine love!"

"You've guessed it, Herr Dagobert."

"It was not a special piece of deduction."

"I tried to reassure myself, but I thought I perceived that Andor had something else on his mind. And then it came out, and that was something more unusual. The object of his worship was—my wife. You look shocked, dear Dagobert. Do not be. I can assure you that I did not lose my mind over this news myself. Only one thing worried me, the fear of being the annoyingly comical figure that the husband is, who is always the last to find such things out, when the whole world was already talking about them. Fortunately, it was not so."

"Thank God!"

"You will have to take back your sigh of relief, dear Dagobert. The facts themselves were fully correct, but luckily, nothing had yet reached the public. That was the main thing, but for the rest I was sitting nicely in it! Still, never for a moment was I doubtful about how I had behaved and what I had done. You might not agree with me, and when I asked around, perhaps no one else would have done it, but I mean, no one who isn't in my position can understand completely. Sometimes situations occur in life where everyone stands by himself and must act according to his own more or less stupid understanding. But I took the Baron to my house. You disapprove?"

"I refrain from judgment, Your Excellency, since I suppose you had your good reasons."

"I was, and I am, convinced that they were sufficient. As to my wife, I have never stopped for a moment to ponder whether she is guilty or not. That was completely indifferent to me and did not interest me. I knew that I would not put it past her. We are long alienated, and if I have not for a long time put an end to it, it was for the sake of the useless talk of the world, and because I did not want to give the great clan of my kinship the satisfaction. They had wanted to hold me back with ropes, when I took a second wife, who was much too young for me, and on top of that from the theater. In fact, from the choir. It was a great stupidity of mine, but I think that every human being has the right to commit a great stupidity in life. For my part, however, I have made a somewhat immodest use of this human right. Our fine agreement had not even lasted a year. I have not, of course, condescended to any disputes. We simply went our own ways. And as for the baron, where should I begin? Duel with him? Doing so, I would have been shouting it from the rooftops, and my name was too good for that. So, I continued to play the role of the unsuspecting benefactor. However, I was not of the opinion that perhaps his sense of honor and conscience should be stirred. I know that there is little reluctance in a man who is in the erotic spell. There was nothing else to be done with him. My request had already been made. I could not leave him at the bank. This would certainly drive him to a greater fraud. If it had to be, it was better perpetrated with me than there. I could have provided him with money and sent him to America, but the big question was whether he would have left! I took him into my service, so I had him under my eyes at least."

"And then the theft was effected promptly!"

"Not quite the way you think, Herr Dagobert. He may be complicit, of course, but it was my wife who stole."

"Is that possible?"

"I must tell you that my wife has been missing since this morning."

"That is terrible!"

"You need not be so horrified, dear friend. The story leaves me quite cold."

"I must confess, Excellency, I am more and more at a loss!"

"I can imagine that you do not understand me yet. It will come."

"But you do not want to have your wife pursued?"

"Do not think of it."

"I think so too. You have got rid of them—thank God and be glad!"

"I am, too."

"So, I'd like to know why I'm actually sitting here. Looking at the whole situation, the most sensible thing seems to be not to stir a finger."

"But you do not know the whole situation yet, and indeed your assistance is most urgently needed. Let me tell you more. Yes, I once did a great stupidity, but I am not so stupid as to have let the two pull the wool over my eyes. I had ordered Andor to become their confidant. He became it. I would not have needed him to learn very soon that an escape had been planned. Once knew this, the course was set for my further plans. To escape, you need money, cash. I had to consider that. The most convenient opportunity was my cashbox, which you see here. The door opposite leads to my bedroom. I had to prepare this opportunity, because I could ignore it and so best protect myself from other unforeseen surprises. I neatened up my cashbox, and one evening, when I knew my wife was observing me, I put inside it a packet of large banknotes. It came to pass what I had expected. The box was opened at night, the money was counted and—was found to be inadequate."

"How could Your Excellency be certain about this?"

"In a very simple way. The contents of my box could only be reached with the help of my keys, not otherwise. These keys—there are three of them—lie on my night stand during the night. I had laid them so that they formed a right-angled triangle, and close to one of the keys was a piece of cigarette ash, which had to be crushed when someone reached for the keys. The next morning the keys did not form a right-angled triangle, and the ashes were crushed."

"My compliments, Your Excellency! I see you would be a top-notch detective!"

"I do not deserve the praise. I first got the idea when I once previously heard a faint clank on the marble slab of my night stand. My wife, the woman of the house, had already peeked before."

"You said, Excellency, that the money had been re-counted?"

"Yes, I had marked the position of the package with two tiny pencil strokes. The next morning, it was no longer within the boundaries."

"Excellent!"

"It was too little for them. By God, I wanted to be sparing, and first tried it with a hundred thousand crowns. I admit that I did wrong. This does not allow for a flight befitting one's rank. I let a few days pass, and then again I put in two hundred and forty thousand crowns. One wants to do things in style!"

"And that was enough?"

"It was enough. This time, my calculation had not left me in the lurch. When I woke up this morning, my keys were once again not in the triangle, the money had disappeared, and so too had my wife and my private secretary, Baron Goth. I was completely satisfied."

"I am very pleased with the philosophical equanimity with which Your Excellency takes things, but I still do not understand what I am to do with them. For the sake of God, you don't want to have them pursued, do you?"

"Certainly, I will, I must."

"Allow me to discourage that most gravely."

"It must be. Of course, I do not want to have my money, my wife, or that gem of a secretary back again. It's a matter of something quite different, far more important."

"I've already guessed, Excellency. For from what I have hitherto heard, and especially from the circumstance that these events have not been able to bring Your Excellency out of spiritual balance, it indicates that you yourself attach a catastrophic significance to it."

"Quite right, dear Dagobert. The most important thing is still to come. So far, I look as if I had survived with all desirable equanimity, right?"

"I can only confirm, from my professional point of view, that the matter was excellently done."

"And yet I've been an ass, my dear Dagobert, and I've committed a colossal stupidity again. However, I also have an excuse for that. Why wouldn't I? In my safe, there was also a golden box, the possession of which is more valuable to me than my life. That is also gone! You will ask how I could be so careless. The box had been there for years. I had become so used to it that I often did not even think about it when I opened the safe. Habit dulls. Besides, I had been so dazed by my clever plans for my liberation that I no longer thought of the greatest treasure I had to guard. That is the only explanation I can offer."

"I assume again, Your Excellency, that it is not the material value that makes you feel the loss so hard."

"I would not have wasted a word about the material value. You can imagine that such a thing does not matter where the final separation from a woman is concerned. Moreover, I have absolutely no idea of the material value that comes into question here. I do not even know if the box contains a document or anything else of value, I only know that I'd rather lose ten million, yes, my whole fortune, than this box."

"Strange! And this box is to be recovered?"

"At all costs! No price is too high."

"Forgive the question, but has Your Excellency apprised Mr. Skrinsky of the disappearance of this box?"

"Of course not! What are you thinking! No one knew, and does not know till this hour, and no one should ever know anything about this box. My beloved wife may have suspected it to contain the jewels of my deceased first wife. This was a fatal mistake for me. As much as I regretted the loss, I would have gotten over it, and would never have bothered the authorities or asked for your services. At most, I would have tried to find the opportunity to buy it back. Skrinsky, I only informed him in order to at least be able to spearhead something for me, in the very worst eventuality, that I should not like to survive, namely, that I did not get the box back at all or not intact, so that I had left nothing untried."

"I understand that, Your Excellency. It is evidently not a question of property, but of a deposit, of entrusted property."

"Certainly like that, but not about the entrusted good in the ordinary sense. It may indeed be replaceable, but I would be free from all sorrows if this loss were replaceable. Skrinsky only knows of the stolen money and the disappeared secretary, and he has the task of seizing the person and belongings of the secretary. Be assured, Herr Dagobert, he will not solve this problem."

"I was not worried, Your Excellency."

"He cannot solve it under the circumstances. When I noticed the loss of the box, my first thought was, "Dagobert must come!""

"Very kind, Your Excellency, but unfortunately, I must again regret the loss of very precious hours!"

"I can also calm you about that. We have not missed anything, and so far, absolutely nothing could be done. I myself would not be able to chat with you here so calmly, if I did not know that there was no danger in progress. Now, however, at any moment, I suspect in an hour at most, the time will come, since our—or rather your—activity will be needed. I am first expecting a message, which I knew could not arrive before the late afternoon. I had time, and I used it. First, I came to an agreement with my friend Grumbach because of you, as to whether I should turn to you."

"But, Excellency—"

"Then it was important to me to arrange the necessary business matters immediately. The personal thing between me and my wife is done. We will not meet each other again in our lives. I had only to ensure her material existence. They may perhaps regard this after the event as an exaggerated care. Even if there should be a reproach in this, I take it quietly. She bears my name. The world will never know anything about the true situation. The countess will always be traveling abroad, for she is no longer allowed to enter the country. Initially, one will wonder in society about this lust for travel. Later, one will get used to it, or think it is for my sake. Our marriage is not resolvable, and thus, appearance is maintained as well as possible. I did not hesitate for long on how to arrange the material side. I imagined how I would have said goodbye to a girlfriend as a gentleman. One has one's "moral" obligations. I did not take her fault into account, and took into account the fact that the lady, who is regarded as the wife of Count Anzbach, also has to live as befitting her standard. I could not give her a capital in her hand with due regard for her own security. She will therefore receive regular monthly allowances until the end of her life from the Central Bank. Here, you can see the duplicate of the form which I have handed over to the bank for handling the details."

He took a document from his desk, which he handed to Dagobert, who read it with great attention.

"The dispositions are wise, and, as was to be expected, exceedingly magnanimous," said Dagobert, returning the document. His Excellency had scarcely placed this in the drawer again when the telephone on his desk gave a faint signal.

"This is most likely the expected news," said the count, with a painfully maintained calm. "Please take an earphone!"

Dagobert did so, and listened in on the following conversation: "Hello, Anzbach here! Who's that?"

"Andor here."

"Thank God! And?"

"I obediently report, Excellency, that we have arrived safely in Salzburg, and have settled in the Hotel Elisabeth."

"Have there been any incidents on the journey?"

"The journey has gone smoothly, Your Excellency."

"Where did you have lunch?"

"In Linz, Your Excellency, at the Hotel Krebs."

"Do you know anything about further travel plans?"

"In service, Excellency. Only an eight-day stay in the Salzkammergut, then onward to Paris."

"What is planned for tomorrow?"

"To drive to St. Gilgen, stay there for two days, at the Seehotel."

"Under what name do they travel?"

"The nobles travel as Count and Countess Aggstein,

so that the crown and initials on the car match."

"What are you doing now?"

"The lady and gentleman are dressing."

"Can you call me again in half an hour, without being noticed?"

"I can, Excellency, as the lady and gentleman wish to take a walk around the city."

"Good, thank you. Keep your eyes open! Goodbye!"

"You see, my dear friend," resumed Count Anzbach to Dagobert, "that up to now nothing could be done, as I did not know the travel route. Now, at last, we can make a decision. For the time being, however, I still owe you some clarification. How it is that Andor travels with them, you will probably be able to piece together. As I foresaw, the flight, I also did what was necessary to prepare it properly. They took my best automobile and my best chauffeur. They consider this to be their stroke of genius. It was mine. They are officially traveling under my eyes. We now know where they will be in the next two days. What do you advise?"

"I still cannot advise at all, Excellency, I only know that I will use tonight's train to get to St. Gilgen. The rest, to put it as Homer did, is in the lap of the gods."

"You will oblige me to inexpressible thanks!"

"Above all, let us set my task. Your Excellency wishes to recover the possession of the box. Otherwise I have nothing to worry about?"

"Otherwise absolutely nothing!"

"And the price does not matter?"

"You have a completely free hand, as far as you want to or must go. I repeat, there is no price too high for me, and I admit to you quite open-heartedly that I would unquestionably sacrifice human life and load blood guilt upon myself if I could not get hold of the box again."

"Now I would doubly and triply dearly like to prevent that, Your Excellency!"

"And another thing, my dear Herr Dagobert! I must have the box returned intact, unopened!"

"Excellency, that is more than a man can promise! Who will vouch for us that the box has not already been opened? That is not unlikely. For they must certainly have been curious to know what they had in their hands."

"It's not that easy to open up. You can see for yourself. Here I have a replica of the box."

He took it from the same desk drawer from which he previously had taken the bank document, and presented it.

"Study this well," he continued. "It will also be useful to insure that you are not given the incorrect box, if negotiations should occur. The solid and very strong iron wall of the box is covered on all sides with a delicate gold decoration in filigree. This covering consists in total of six hundred small, finely worked rosettes in the rococo style. In the middle of each rosette you see a small hole. In each of these holes fits the key to the box, which may not be unlike an old-fashioned watch-key, I assume. For I myself never saw it. It still lies, as it was given to me, in a sealed envelope in my safe box. They overlooked to take it with them, or more correctly, they did not guess the key was in the envelope. But even if they had taken the key with them, it would have been useless without knowledge of how to use it. For greater security, I also kept the 'Instructions for Use' elsewhere in a sealed envelope, fire- and burglar-proof. I mean to tell you the secret, but it will not do any good to you without the instructions."

"Even so, it is of interest to me, Your Excellency," said Dagobert.

"Good. We have here six hundred exactly identical key-holes, and only seven of them count. Without instruction, no person can know which they are. With a lot of testing, you could discover one correct one or another—you would not get anywhere. The seven tiny, but very strong locks inside the box only give when opened in the correct order. Thus, someone should then try out six hundred key holes and find the only correct order in the decisive holes. You know, I am not a great mathematician, but I can imagine without a protracted calculation that there are so many permutations that one would have to try for a few million years to arrive at the right solution."

"A very strange little box!"

"It was the anniversary gift to a high-ranking person

from the cooperatives of the goldsmiths and art locksmiths. And since we are now so far along, dear Dagobert, you should also know everything, so that you can fully understand the importance that this matter has for me. You will not be unaware of what all the world knows and gossips about, that I enjoy the distinction of being honored by that figure with unreserved trust. Every man, whether high or low, has something in his life that he does not want to shout from the rooftops. My friend has the wish that in the event of his death, a matter which is dear to him will be settled by me in silence according to his will, without much being said about it and consulting all sorts of unbidden authorities and commissions. So, a secret and a last will, laid down in my hands with a touching, friendly confidence, and now I am supposed to go and say, 'This is how I have justified your confidence! Your secret is now, through my fault, in the hands of riff-raff, who will scream it over all the rooftops tomorrow if it promised to be of use!' You see, dear Dagobert, how serious the matter is. Do you think it possible that I would step forward with such a confession? Do you now believe that in the event of a critical emergency, the life of the two inferior people, who are still amusing themselves uncontested while they are escaping, will be more valuable to me than the secret entrusted to me? Every last will is said to be holy, and this is to me threefold and tenfold. Can you believe that my own life—Oh, I do not need to finish. There are things about which one does not speak because they are self-evident."

"Thank you, Your Excellency, for entrusting me with this. I only now fully grasp the meaning of my task. The little box, therefore, we can safely assume, has not yet been opened. It could not be unlocked. There is nothing to be done by force, not so easily at least. It is questionable whether these fine steel walls can also be overcome with a heavy wood chopper. Without a commotion, such an attempt would not be possible. They may also have lacked the proper opportunity to date. And besides, one does not tackle such a wonderful masterpiece of the goldsmithing art with such brutal means. One would rather leave time, especially since a lack of money cannot yet have spurred their curiosity on. Fine instruments, drills, saws and even crowbars would not work there. They would be caught in the deed, as trained international burglars are sometimes found with such tools. And trained burglars our two pleasure-travelers are not. I therefore venture to hope that the box is still intact, and that it will be possible to bring the business to a fruitful conclusion. Now, Your Excellency, I would just like to ask you a few questions."

"Please, ask, Dagobert."

"Are you quite sure you can rely on Andor?"

"Absolutely! As sure as I'm sitting here. Andor is an abnormal case who simply does not fit into our time. If I give him the order today that those two people are not allowed to survive tomorrow, then you can be sure that they will not survive it. That is the only thing that reassures me somewhat."

"Does Andor know anything about the box?"

"Not a syllable. I only made the terrible discovery after the departure. But I will inform him by telephonic means."

"I would ask you, Excellency, not to do so. Communicating by phone is difficult and unsafe. One has no guarantee whether somehow, somewhere, someone is listening to the conversation. As little as possible, preferably nothing at all, is to be said of the box. In any case, I will be there early tomorrow morning. I would be glad if Excellency had already informed Andor that He wanted him to be absolutely at my disposal."

"He will be at your disposal, Herr Dagobert, and you can count on him to do all your orders, whatever their nature, on time. For the rest, of course, it is also preferable to me –you can imagine—that no superfluous word should be spoken about the entire matter."

"Then we agree, Excellency, and now I would like to ask for an explanation. How does the matter really relate to this second box? One glance has already taught me that this box cannot be an exact replica. In fact, it has only one lock and that has nothing mysterious about it."

Count Anzbach laughed.

"How you notice everything, dear Dagobert! One can see you are a professional! I was not, indeed, given two identical boxes, not two at all. The matter is like this: when I received the original, I was so delighted that I immediately resolved to have a copy made. I went to Friedinger, the Court goldsmith, who had procured the ornamental furnishing, and asked him to make me a copy. At first, he had all sorts of misgivings, but I could easily dispel them, especially as I did not put the slightest weight on the most delicate point, the artistic closure. I merely was charmed by the decorative art. Friedinger knew who he was dealing with, and so I could implement what no one else could have done."

"It is a masterpiece and a true *pièce de résistance*! I thus estimate its worth at about fourteen thousand crowns."

"I paid sixteen thousand for it, and I certainly did not overpay."

"Certainly not! Would you now trust me with your box, Your Excellency? It may be useful for me to study it."

"Not only do I entrust you, dear Dagobert, I would have liked to make it a present to you, as a token of friendship—if we had not been so imprudent as to discuss the price."

"Many thanks, Your Excellency, but as a gift it would have been too precious for me. You know I'm an amateur in my field, and am not impelled by cash prizes, nor even for honorary prizes that could be viewed as a substitute for the money. So, I may take the box?"

"Here you have it. Incidentally, Andor might now - oh, *lupus in fabula*! There he is reporting back again."

In fact, the Count had been interrupted by a soft signal in mid-sentence. He invited Dagobert to listen again.

"Hello, Anzbach here!"

"At your orders, Your Excellency, this is Andor."

"Is there anything new?"

"Nothing of importance, Excellency. The lady and gentleman have gone out."

"Are they still going to go to St. Gilgen tomorrow?"

"At your service, Excellency, I have already ordered apartments by telephone, and I am assured that everything will be ready."

"Good. Now listen, Andor, what I say. Sitting by my telephone is a gentleman who is my friend. He wishes to speak to you at once. Before that, I will only tell you that he is on the point of doing for me a very important service out of friendship. He will look for you, but you must not make yourself conspicuous. If he commands you, you must obey blindly, as if I had given them. Did you understand me?"

"At your command, Your Excellency."

"Now listen, the gentleman will talk to you himself."

"Hello, Herr Andor," began Dagobert, "when do you plan to leave tomorrow?"

"If you please, at ten o'clock. Dinner is ordered at the Seehotel in St. Gilgen for one o'clock."

"I'll wait for you outside the Seehotel."

"Please bring a special mark or password."

"A password is sufficient. Let's say — 'Mercedes.' This will not be conspicuous with a chauffeur."

"At your command, 'Mercedes!'"

"Fine. Now tell me: how does it stand with the luggage of the lady and gentleman? How many pieces do they have with them, and how is it transported?"

"We've got three: two suitcases, and a travelling basket that I carry on the car. The lady and gentleman have only taken the most necessary items for the journey. It is only in Paris that new things will be purchased."

"All right, Herr Andor, only one more request: be very careful to ensure that nothing gets away from the luggage. I have nothing more to say for the moment. Goodbye until tomorrow. Thank you. Goodbye!"

"So, you really want to travel?" Count Anzbach again took command.

"Of course, tonight by the express night train. So, Your Excellency, I have your authority?"

"My unlimited authority. Word and handshake on it. You know what is at stake for me. I am not petty anyway, and I will not be in this case for God's sake. But wouldn't you rather use one of my automobiles for the journey? You will travel more comfortably and certainly no less quickly."

"Thank you very much, Your Excellency, but I will take the train. I must be on the spot tomorrow morning. A car can suffer a breakdown, then there are also still unlit railway barriers, those confounded nuisances for motorists. I must not expose myself to an accident. The railway is safer. By the way, my automobile will be traveling the same journey at the same time. This is in case I should be compelled to pursue the lady and gentleman from St. Gilgen, in order to keep them in sight inconspicuously, and yet constantly."

With this Dagobert took his leave, accompanied by the blessings of his client.

***

The next day passed without Count Anzbach receiving a message, but the next morning, at nine o'clock, his private secretary Erdmann informed him that the head waiter from the Seehotel was asking to be received by His Excellency. The applicant was immediately admitted.

"What news do you bring?" The count said, hastily, whose voice trembled from the tremendous excitement from which he suffered.

The man looked at him and remained in silence. The Count understood. First, the secretary must retire. But he had scarcely closed the door behind him than the question was repeated in full impatience. The answer was: "I have the honor to report to Your Excellency that the task has been accomplished."

Count Anzbach grabbed his head and then burst into uproarious laughter.

"Upon my soul, Herr Dagobert, how you have disguised yourself!"

"As I must, Your Excellency. Really, I did not like to do it."

"I would not have recognized you in all my life!"

"I feel very flattered, Excellency. I was already flattered when your private secretary did not recognize me."

"And the main thing—did it succeed?"

"Completely. You may be assured, Excellency. Here is the box. It is intact, and we know that it could not have been opened."

Dagobert had taken the mysterious box from the expansive cape that he wore over his waiter's tails, and handed it over to the Count, who took it with trembling hands, and immediately established its authenticity, and heaved a deep sigh of salvation. His voice was trembling with inner emotion as he expressed his thanks.

"I take the matter, Herr Dagobert, as if you had saved my life. For I really did not know how I should continue to live if—Oh, thank God, a thousand times! I absolutely do not wish to think about that anymore. But now, Herr Dagobert—but what is this nonsense of 'Herr Dagobert' and 'Count', between us? A man who has done this for me is my friend for life, is my brother. Go on, Dagobert, tell me all about it."

"The matter was not as difficult as you might

imagine, Your Excellency. I should almost like to say 'alas.'"

"Not difficult—for you! The way you have disguised yourself is a work of art in itself."

"Such small pieces of artifice must occasionally go hand-in-hand with the detective craft, and you cannot, of course, bungle it, or it will only make things worse."

In fact, Dagobert had metamorphosed quite masterfully. In the shabbily elegant dress suit, his figure appeared much slimmer than usual. His face was clean-shaven, and his head adorned with a blonde wig that was parted behind, while in front, the sparse bangs were brushed over his forehead, which thus appeared very low and gave the whole visage a stupid expression that inspired confidence.

"It will take weeks," remarked Dagobert, painfully smiling, "before I return to my usual beauty. So listen, here's how it went. When I left you the evening before last, I had to take care of various matters. Preparations had to be made for the smooth conduct of my activity. At first, I had a certain plan in mind, but I did not rely solely upon it from the outset. If this failed, something else had to be tried. So, I telephoned to Salzburg to one of my pupils, who there had enjoyed ample opportunity of prosperous and meritorious activity in the strong tourist sector."

"Have you pupils, too, Dagobert?"

"A great many. In fact, I have the honor of leading a class in the detective school of our criminal investigation department. Many of my most gifted students are already quite successful at their work, scattered around the world. I told the Salzburg man— his name is Schaffler—that I was going to St. Gilgen that same evening, and to secure the two rooms on either side of the rooms arranged for the fleeing couple. I did not need to give elaborate explanations to a specialist like him. He understood immediately, and promised at the same time to provide unobtrusive holes in the connecting doors for the purpose of observation. That was my plan, too. If necessary, he had to watch out on the one side, I on the other. But I still had to take care of something more important. I had to create the opportunity to enter the chambers of the lady and gentleman as I pleased, without attracting any notice. There was only one way to do that: I had to be their room waiter. No easy thing. The reigning head waiter had to be dismissed for this purpose. I did not want to entrust this mission to Schaffler, with all due respect for his abilities. He would have had to negotiate with the hotel proprietor and the head waiter, and although I thought I could trust him, I was not sure whether a careless or malicious word by one or other of them might spoil everything. I had to take care of it myself, and I did so."

"You old fox, Dagobert! How did you do that?"

"Already dressed as head waiter, as you see me now, I went to see the hotel owner. In the office I locked the door behind me and asked him, so as not to have to speak too loudly, to call a certain Viennese telephone number.

"'But,'" he cried in astonishment, "'that's the number of...!'

"'Quite right,' I interrupted. 'You needn't say the name. Your call is expected.'

He called and received the instructions to fulfill my orders unconditionally and without delay. Even for the slightest omission, he would be made personally responsible! The effect was an amazing one. He immediately put himself at my disposal unconditionally."

"Who then is the one who is able to exercise such a power?"

"A person who stays every summer at the Seehotel, and has every cause to think highly of the owner. Let me conceal the name. One has one's connections, but in my profession, it is no good to name-drop conceitedly. In short, a person whose will is done, and whom one does not contradict."

"Right. Vacationing in St. Gilgen—now I know who it was, without a doubt! It is no wonder, of course! My compliments, Dagobert, for the idea"

"I was sure of the owner. Now the head waiter had to be moved out of the way. I had him come, pressed a hundred-crown note in his hand, and, without giving him the opportunity to speak to anyone, put him in my car, which had meanwhile also arrived, informed him that he would now be going on a beautiful outing. My chauffeur was commissioned to take him to Berchtesgaden. The weather was not quite suitable for a country outing—the typical constant, heavy Salzburg rain—simply ugly, but I could do nothing about it. That was his bad luck."

"Boldly done, I must say!"

"Now I was certainly master of the situation. Schaffler had fulfilled my orders well, and, so that he would not be seen unnecessarily, was interned in one of the two side rooms, so as to be able to move into his observation post immediately. And now comes the humor of the matter. The lady and gentleman who had made their escape under your auspices were received in the hotel also under your auspices. As they drove up, I received them. I asked the chauffeur in an incidental manner with an expert look at the car: Mercedes? His eyes widened, but he kept to the plan. I accompanied the lady and gentleman into their apartments, supervised the transport of their luggage from the car, and made sure that they were served in everything as befits those who travel under your auspices."

"This gentle respect honors me."

"They drove up at twelve o'clock. Dinner was ordered for one o'clock. They immediately went to wash up and change, so I had time to exchange a few words with Andor. Nothing remarkable had happened in the meantime, but something Andor reported caused me a lot of unease and worried me greatly. With regard to the miserable beastly weather, they had changed their travel plans. They'd had enough of the Salzkammergut lake district. They wanted to return to a city as soon as possible, and the next destination was Munich. Immediately after dinner, the journey was to resume. For me it was now: *Hic Rhodus, hic salta!* Here and now I had to finish the thing. I had hardly another chance. For I had already, as I am now obliged to see, made a great stupidity, which must prevent me from continuing to hold on to their heels. They had already seen me! That was crucial. To use a further disguise—such a thing is, at best, for sensational novellas or gothic dramas calculated for a naive audience. A rational man in the field cannot be put to such a position. The predicament into which I had fallen was, in fact, not at all unwelcome. It called for a quick decision, and when something is urgent, one's thoughts are better focused. I had to adapt to the circumstances and finish my plan."

"Happy Dagobert, who always thinks of something!"

"The lady and gentleman were dressing for dinner. They wanted to have it served in the dining room, where a festively laid table was ready for them. That was the opportunity, the only one that offered itself to me. I set off for the room reserved for myself, but did not spend much time watching them, especially since I had noticed that they were in no rush to dress, so rather, I sat down quietly and wrote a letter. I had time."

"Such composure!"

"When the gongs proclaimed that it was dinner time, they left their rooms, which they shut behind them, and now I entered them from my room. Beforehand, I had instructed Andor to watch them from a safe distance at dinner, and, if they were to leave early unexpectedly, to signal me with two blasts of the car's horn. Of course, I had also set Schaffler in the stairwell, who also was to inform me by means of an agreed sign if there was danger afoot. So, I could operate in a tolerable security. I was prepared to open the suitcases with my tools, if necessary. In my profession one must understand such things. But it was not necessary. The suitcases had not been relocked. Of course, I began with the Countess's suitcase. In two minutes the matter had been settled. I had the box."

"Be blessed a thousand times!"

"But I could not be content with it. There was the possibility that the loss of the box would be noticed immediately before departure, and it was not at all clear what might have happened then. This was a danger which had to be prevented. I prevented it."

"And how did you manage that, Dagobert?"

"I had taken the second box, and now deposited the copy in place of the original. No one could tell the difference. I got our treasure to safety, and the lady and gentleman had not yet eaten their soup when I was with them again, and watched with all due care that they were served flawlessly. They were also very satisfied, and when they set off for their further journey immediately after dinner, I helped to bring down the luggage—they had not even taken an afternoon nap— and I enjoyed the good fortune of receiving a piece of gold as a generous tip. I am proud of this gold coin, and I will carry it as a souvenir on my watch-chain. I think it's as good as a medal."

"It will also be a reminder for me, Dagobert, whenever I see you, how much thanks I owe you!"

"Of course, they had paid for the apartment for two days without objecting. My surprise coup raised a question of justice, whether I could act like that. I didn't worry about it for long. In no other case, perhaps, would I have behaved like this. Here, there was no question of any definable value. Any negotiations could fail, offers, however brilliant they were, could be categorically rejected, but the box I had to have. It was an exceptional case. I accept responsibility for it."

"And of course I will, too!"

"The countess will never know the true facts. She will most likely not bother with the box until she's in Paris, firstly, because she hasn't been able open it. The copy is locked, as well, and naturally I didn't leave her the key, but this box will ultimately be easy to open. She will not become suspicious, and she will not suspect the room waiter of St. Gilgen, whom she has only seen so fleetingly. By the time she gets to Paris, she will have been in so many hotels, and have met so many waiters that she will barely remember Jean of St. Gilgen."

"If it had been up to me, Dagobert, you could easily have put money or precious jewels in the box."

"I have deposited something else, Your Excellency, and I believe I acted according to your wishes. The countess, when she finally opens the box, will experience a sensual surprise."

"A surprise?" asked Excellency.

"Yes, a delicate, sensual surprise, which might cause her somewhat of a headache. It is impossible for you to ever come into contact with her again. Now it was necessary, however, to bring her some knowledge. I have now taken care of that. She will find a letter in the box."

"A letter?"

"As follows—please allow me, Excellency to read you my draft copy. You can hardly decipher my scribbling. So:

Your Excellency, dear Countess!

As Your Excellency intends to travel suddenly, and seems to have the desire to surprise His Excellency, and as he himself does not wish to interfere with your esteemed enterprise by personal intervention, he entrusts me to give you, in this way, in his name, best wishes for a happy trip. At the same time, I have the honor of informing Your Excellency, in his name that, of course, His Excellency has already ensured that as long as you remain abroad, you will never lack the means to live a proper life, according to your station. The Central Bank is charged with satisfying your wishes and needs with the greatest punctuality, I emphasize again: as long as you live abroad.

Allow me, Your Excellency, to join the wishes of His Excellency, and to wish you a happy journey, from my heart, with which I have the honor of signing as

Your very devoted Dagobert.

Well, Your Excellency, do you agree?"

"Famously done, Dagobert! At least they do not have the satisfaction of thinking that we are the dupes."

Count Anzbach was too tactful to express his deep-felt gratitude to Dagobert in any tangible way. But Dagobert was very happy when, a few days later, he was complimented publicly on receiving a high distinction. In the Official Gazette, it was noted that he had been awarded the Order of the Iron Crown.

The Publisher

You think this is another short story, don't you? Well, you are half-right. We've included the prologue of our upcoming mystery novel, *Death in a Bookstore* (available in January 2018) by the famous Italian author Augusto De Angelis. We hope you enjoy it. But first, a word from our sponsor, which is us!

Kazabo Publishing is a new idea in the literary world. Our motto is, "Every Book a Best Seller . . . Guaranteed!" And we mean it. Our mission is to find best-selling books from around the world that, for whatever reason, have not been published in English. The book of short stories by Luigi Capuana that you have just read, for example, has been immensely popular in Europe, particularly in Italy, for over a hundred years. Why has it never been published in English before? We don't know. But we think you will agree that it should have been. And now it is.

We have found there are also many contemporary writers who are very popular in their own countries but who have not made it into English. We think this is a real shame so we are working to bring those books and those authors to you.

When you visit Kazabo.com (our website!), we hope

you will always discover something new, either a book from a favorite author you didn't know existed or a completely new author with a fresh perspective from a country you admire. We promise you that everything you see with the Kazabo name – even authors you have never heard of – will be a best-seller; maybe in Italy, maybe in Japan, maybe in 1902, but a best seller. We hope you enjoy reading these literary gems as much as we enjoy finding them and bringing them to you.

But enough about us. Here is an excerpt from our upcoming mystery novel by Augusto De Angelis, *Death in a Bookstore*.

Thanks for reading!

The Kazabo Team

Kazabo.com

Death in a Bookstore

By Augusto De Angelis

Prologue

Please deliver to the police station.

He contemplated the bundle lying on the steps of the church.

The early light of dawn illuminated the deserted square. Under the entrance corridor, which led to an open courtyard, the sunrise lit up the image of the Madonna. A few minutes before, all the streetlights had turned off suddenly. The air was chilly.

A new day was born in the big city, which remained nearly motionless. The noise of trams could be heard in the distance, on Corso Vittorio Emanuele, and on the other side, Via Cavallotti.

The man in the gray uniform looked at the bundle.

It must be rags wrapped up in newspaper, he thought. Yet the parcel appeared too carefully packaged to contain rags.

He hit it with the broom and the bundle rolled down the stairs onto the pavement. It didn't open. It had to be closed with some pin, because it was not tied. From the center of the bundle, below the newspaper's edge, a white envelope appeared.

The sweeper bent to reach the envelope. It was open. It contained a piece of paper folded in fourths. Upon the paper was scrawled a message in large and hurried script in blue ink. *"Please deliver to the police station."*

In his eyes, the parcel had now gained importance. He looked at it with respect , even a little fear. Whatever was wrapped in that newspaper, now that he had found it, he had the irritating responsibility of going to the San Fedele Police station to deliver it. After that would come the even bigger nuisance to be questioned, give explanations, repeat them in court... He knew how it worked! Once he had picked up a bunch of fake tickets, and due to that experience he cursed counterfeiters around the world.

So many things had happened to him! In twenty years as a street sweeper, he had found nothing but rubbish and trouble on the ground.

He looked around. There was nobody.

He kicked the package, which rolled farther. But it was not so light, because it didn't go too far.

Sighing, he passed the back of his hand over his mouth. Finally, he picked up the parcel. There were two pins, in fact, to keep the folds of the newspaper closed around the parcel. He touched the bundle. It was soft; there were certainly garments inside. Still, there was something hard in the middle of the garments, which weighed more.

He approached the empty cart, and placed the package on the closed lid. He secured the broom on the two side hooks and put the letter inside his pocket. He grabbed the rods and pushed the cart. He started slowly down Via Pasquirolo, toward Piazza Beccaria, the iron cart resonated on the pavement.

When he arrived at San Fedele, it was broad daylight.

He took the long way and stopped in front of the Galleria to buy coffee with grappa from a street vendor. The vendor looked him up and down twice before serving him, as he had never seen him before.

"Are you new here? Who are you replacing?"

"Nobody. I was just passing by."

"Are you taking a stroll with your *Isotta Fraschini*?"

He didn't answer. He didn't want to talk. The story of the bundle to be delivered to police headquarters had put him in a bad mood. He grabbed his *Isotta Fraschini* and left.

At the door of San Fedele, he stopped with the bundle in his hands. Who should he deliver it to?

A *carabiniere* was looking at him.

"Tell me... excuse me..."

"I don't know anything. There, under the porch, there is an agent."

The sweeper addressed the agent, who was smoking.

"I found this on the steps of the church of San Vito, off Via Pasquirolo."

"And you brought it here?! You should know that City Hall takes care of such things..."

"Lost items, yes I know. And you get a ten percent tip, too, when you bring them in. But please, read this!"

He gave him the envelope containing the note.

The agent read it and laughed.

"It's a joke! Have you looked inside?"

"No. I don't want to get in trouble!"

"Why? Is it heavy? You think there's a woman's head cut into pieces inside?!"

And he kept on laughing.

The street sweeper stared at the bundle in his hands in terror. No! It couldn't be someone's head. It was soft. The heavier part was in the middle, but it was too small to be a head.

"Well! Go over there to the Flying Squad. The Inspector is in. The night shift agent must still be asleep."

The sweeper crossed the yard and knocked on a door on which he read: "Flying Squad- Chief Inspector."

A gentle, courteous voice answered him.

"Come in. What's up?"

Inside, he found a brunette young man elegantly dressed, who looked at him with vague eyes. He was still absorbed in some thought or his reading.

"I found this, Inspector... on the steps of San Vito al Pasquirolo..."

"So?"

"There was this letter too."

The inspector read the letter.

"Ok, give it to me."

He took the bundle, removed the pins, looked at them – they were common pins – and opened the newspaper.

A clean, white coat appeared, like those worn by doctors or nurses. The inspector opened the coat and four surgical instruments fell on the table; they were bright, shiny, and sharp.

Nothing else.

The sweeper stood observing.

The inspector took the instruments and examined them one at a time. He recognized a scalpel and then saw some kind of screwdriver, surgical scissors, and a long caliper.

The scalpel had some brown spots. The other tools seemed new.

The inspector rang the bell and a little later the guard appeared.

"Call Sergeant Cruni," he intoned in his courteous voice.

The guard disappeared.

When Cruni arrived, he was still sleepy. He was short and muscular, and his body was too massive for such short legs.

"I am needed, sir?"

"Draw up a report of found objects and register this man's personal data."

"Yes, *Cavaliere*. Please come with me."

Once alone, Inspector De Vincenzi touched the coat, lifted it, and then looked at the surgical instruments. He took up the scalpel and examined it closely.

"Blood stains," he murmured.

He got up and locked everything in the closet.

Then he sat back at his desk and took the book he was reading out of the drawer. It was the last novel by Körmendi. He read all sorts of things.

Almost immediately he looked up from the page and stared at the closet. The piece of paper with the strange request was still on the desk.

Who would abandon four surgical instruments, including a blood-spotted scalpel and a white coat?

He examined the handwritten note. It was written quickly with a fountain pen. It didn't look fake: whoever wrote it was serious. At the very least, they were in a hurry.

He dropped the note on the desk and glanced at the clock: it was almost seven. He began reading aloud, with a bitter smile, the calendar in front of him:

"At 8:30 AM the Sun enters the sign of Aries... and at 2:28 PM Spring begins."

He tore the page from the calendar and March 21 appeared, completely blank.

"Aries..." he murmured again. "If only I believed in horoscopes!"

Then he shrugged. The truth was, he did believe in horoscopes as well as in many more things, including misfortune, telepathy, and premonitions. He was superstitious.

Why did he receive four surgical instruments and a white coat on the very first day of Spring?

What should he do? Nothing, obviously. The letter and the bundle could not force him to do anything, neither as a police inspector nor as a man. But he could think about it, of course.

The newspaper in which they had been wrapped was the *Corriere* of March 20th. He read it and found nothing special. He folded it and put it in the drawer.

In the afternoon, when he came back to his office, he would show the instruments to a doctor to find out more about them. And then he would wait. Nothing else had happened, or maybe something was happening or could have happened already.

Maybe a murder?

No! He closed the book and put it in the drawer, then got up, put on his overcoat, grabbed his hat and, when he reached the door, he turned off the light.

From the arch facing the courtyard, through the dirty railing and the closed, even dirtier windows, a pale daylight came in.

De Vincenzi sighed. He had become accustomed to going to bed when the sun was already high, for he spent most nights at the police station, working or reading. Yet, he sighed every morning. Because every morning, at the sight of the new day, he thought of the country house, in the Ossola, where he was born, and where his mother still lived, with the hens, the dogs and the maid. He would have been so glad to join his mother. He was young, not even thirty-five, yet he felt old. He had fought in the war. And he had a contemplative spirit. Some of his boarding school mates called him a poet to make fun of him. He was so much a poet, that he became a police inspector...

He was about to open the door to leave when the phone rang. He winced. Why now?!

THE END (Really!)

Made in the USA
San Bernardino, CA
03 March 2018